0

Acknowledgements

Grateful thanks to a patient husband and daughter.

Names of people and places are entirely fictitious and any likeness is illusory.

SUSPICION

PROLOGUE

The back bedroom in the large semi-detached house in Broad Lane is a shambles. Drawers hang out and wardrobe doors stand open revealing their hidden secrets. Panties and bras, nighties and tights mingle with makeup, hair adornments, purses and scarves strewn in rainbow abandon over the lush cream carpet. The duvet is pushed back on the bed, the bottom sheet showing several streaks of bloodstain.

A girl stands before the dressing table. She is naked. Staring in the triple mirror where she can view her body from all angles, she feels the nausea swim over her and the bile rise in her throat. Across her shoulders and buttocks are several red weals oozing blood-stained sticky moisture. Bruises and bite marks cover her breasts, the nipples raw and seeping. More angry bruising shows on her upper arms and inner thighs. Her eyes are puffy and red from weeping and the face that stares back at her is white and haunted. A spreading bruise distorts her left cheek like a birthmark. Grabbing her dressing gown from the bed she hobbles into the bathroom and retches into the toilet basin. Holding the washbowl, she mops her face and stares in the bathroom mirror.

"Oh God, what am I going to do?" she beseeches her reflection, misery and fear clouding her brown eyes.

"I can't stay here any longer and I can't go out looking like this, I'm so sore I can hardly move. I can't face school today but tomorrow, I'm going away. I'm leaving here."

CHAPTER ONE. THE CRIME.

It is Tuesday morning and Tom Prescott is towelling his long, lean body, engrossed, revelling in the feeling of well-being the activity produces. His wife Hazel passes him the telephone round the bathroom door.

"Here's your early morning call," she sings. "Mr Finch for you."

It isn't unusual for the Head, Peter Finch to ring before school commences, but Tom is well organized in the mornings. He rises at six-thirty and goes for a run where his pal Rick joins him. Seven- thirty finds him as now, in the shower before a hearty breakfast at eight a.m. By eight thirty, he is in his form room at the comprehensive school, about two hundred yards distant on the opposite side of the road from his house in the Dales market town of Weyburne.

Peter Finch's brisk voice comes over the line,

"Good morning Mr. Prescott. I want to see you in my office as soon as possible this morning please. Would eight twenty be convenient? Fine. Good."

Tom puts down the phone thoughtfully. It is normal practice for Peter Finch to command the presence of Dick Blendell the Deputy Head, himself as Senior Master and Mrs Beales the Senior Girls Mistress, to an early meeting. Why does it sound different today? This is a definite order with no frills or explanations and an air of tension about it. A ripple of unease courses along Tom's gut. Then he shrugs as he rakes a comb through the wiry tangle of his wet hair. He'll find out soon enough, after the priority of breakfast.

The first meal of the day is usually a high-speed affair with everyone assembling in various stages of alertness and dress. Hazel piles an assortment of cereal packets, butter, marmalade and fruit on the table while she prepares mounds of toast and cooks bacon and eggs for the starving. A small creature winds itself round her legs mewing piteously.

"Poor Mitzy. Are you starving too."

She places a loaded saucer on the floor and the little animal buries its nose in the food making a satisfied purr. This recent addition to the Prescott family is adopted from their milkman who wanted a good home for the grey and white kitten. It is common for Tom to be fed and away before the younger generation appear and it is so this morning. Flinging on his jacket and planting a kiss on Hazel's cheek, he dashes to the door.

"Cheerio love. See you later you lay a beds."

Promptly at the required time, Tom knocks on the door marked 'Headmaster' and is requested to enter.

"Good morning Mr. Prescott, please sit down."

A surprised Tom notices the absence of others. After he is seated, there is a pause during which Peter Finch unsmilingly studies his Senior Master over steepled fingers. The effect of this treatment is unsettling and Tom scrambles into the corners of his mind for possible indiscretions. Uneasiness again stirs his entrails.

"Mr. Prescott, I've something unpleasant to tell you and there is no easy way to say it."

"Whatever it is Headmaster, spit it out. I can take it."

"Mmm, well it's like this. A parent came to see me late last night at home. I deliberated upon whether to call round and see you straight away, and then thought it better to wait until this morning. There was no need for two of us to lose sleep."

Tom is now becoming alarmed. These delaying tactics are out of character for Peter Finch. He usually comes straight to the point.

"Yes Sir?" he prompts.

"He has accused you of laying hands upon his daughter. Fondling her intimately."

Whatever Tom expected could not have winded him like this punch below the belt. He is bomb-clapped. He feels his chin drop and his eyes widen as his intestines coil into knots.

"Who's the girl Sir? Am I allowed to know?"

"Of course. You have that right. The girl's name is Annette Grayson and it's her father, Mr Grayson who came to complain. He's an extremely angry man. He's reporting the alleged incident to the police first thing this morning."

Tom wilts in his chair. He looks at the Head stupidly and manages a hoarse whisper.

"I simply cannot believe this is happening."

Collecting his limbs and brain cells he sits upright in his seat.

"These allegations are completely untrue. I've never touched this girl or any other, except openly and innocently for their own safety or

9

that of others. When's the incident supposed to have happened?"

"Mr. Grayson states she was on the field trip to Whitby last week and you put your arm around her then, but alleges there is another occasion that he wouldn't tell me about."
Peter Finch twiddles with a pencil.

"Tom, could you possibly have touched this girl in any way that might have been misinterpreted?"

"Well Sir, there was the one incident and I mentioned it in my report on the field trip. The whole group were given rules about behaviour, one of which was not going near the cliff edge because of reported landslides in that area. Annette Grayson and Melissa Dean were fooling about on the edge of the cliff top; I put a hand on the shoulder of each girl, pulled them back and tore them off a strip. That's the only occasion I've ever touched her."

"Can you think of any reason she should be making these accusations? Revenge maybe? A dare?"

Tom shrugs his shoulders;

"I can't recall chastising her at all apart from that once. She isn't naughty or unruly. She is however a very troubled girl. I've often felt she wanted to tell me something but couldn't. In fact, last term I suggested she talk to Mrs Beales if she had a problem."

"Did she do that?"

"No Sir, she didn't."

"Have you any idea what her problem is?"

"No Sir. I could make one or two wild guesses bearing in mind her home life, but nothing definite."

"What do know about her home life?"

"Well, her father has the department store in the town and her mother works there full time. Annette's an only child and spends a lot of time at home by herself."

"Yes I see. Well Mr Prescott, I suggest you go home and contact your solicitor without delay."

"I will Sir. What happens now?"

"You will appreciate this is a very serious and sensitive matter. Mr.Grayson refused my suggestion that because of your long and blameless record, we could resolve the matter internally. He insisted on going to the police and I'm afraid it's in their hands."

Peter Finch shrugs his shoulders and puts his pencil in the tray before looking Tom in the eye.

"There was no time even to call a meeting of Governors last night but I'm trying to contact members of the board to arrange one as soon as possible. There will probably be an internal enquiry too."

He again picks up his pencil and doodles something on a scrap of paper.

"Mr Prescott, I have no alternative but to suspend you and as of this moment, you are relieved of all duties. You will of course have your salary paid as usual." He anticipates Tom's questions and adds,

"I shall arrange someone to take over your classes, so you need have no worries in that direction."

He fiddles with his pencil and looks at it thoughtfully.

"We'll have to use a supply teacher for a week or two. Take your personal things and go home now until you hear from me."

Tom looks at his Head blankly. Suspended? Week or two? His brain hasn't cogged on to that possibility.

"Suspension?" he whispers. "That's tantamount to being pronounced guilty."

"No no. In this country everybody is innocent until *proven* guilty. We'll soon have the whole thing cleared up. We cannot afford to lose a good teacher. Go home now." Finch rises quickly to his feet and pushes back his chair.

"You will be contacted by the police this morning and I will inform you if there is to be an enquiry as soon as it's arranged."

Tom gets up and walks to the office door, turning with his hand on the knob as Peter Finch's voice follows him.

"Tom. I cannot tell you how sorry I am this has happened and I want you to know, I do not believe a word of it. To protect every one and in view of the seriousness of the charges, I have to take this step. If there's any way you think I can help you, please call me at any time. I mean that."

Finch is now walking towards Tom. He sees a tall athletic man with curly chestnut hair and ruddy complexion. Shock and anxiety have drained the colour from his cheeks. His eyes are different; one being brown while the other is greeny brown.

"I'm confident all the staff will join me in supporting you. Before school commences this morning, I shall acquaint them with the circumstances of your absence. Good luck Tom."

Peter Finch is grammar school educated and runs his enterprise on as similar lines as permitted within the constraints of OFSTED. Familiarity is discouraged and teachers are referred to by their full title in public at all times. This speech from him now is completely atypical and Tom is surprised and warmed.

Local pupils make their own way into school but children from surrounding villages travel by school bus. The school serves a catchment area of around twenty five miles in each direction and buses begin arriving from 8.45 am.

The school is still quiet as Tom makes his way to his form room to collect his things. His hands move automatically arranging his prepared syllabus, timetables and lesson plans, making things as easy as possible for his stand-in to take over. Where he would normally be full of ideas for the progression of his day, his thoughts leaping ahead to the next hour, the next lesson and the afternoon; he feels brain dead. The anaesthetic of shock has stopped the lively flow of his thoughts. His day and his life have disappeared and he can't see beyond this vast chasm that's opened beneath his feet, threatening to suck him down into its maw. Tom looks at his watch. It is just 8.30 a.m. His world has crashed around him in fifteen minutes.

He turns at the door and looks back at what once was his kingdom, wondering when he will again rule there. The tidy rows of tables with chairs tucked under, stand empty now. The white board, shelves laden with books, fossils and other relics, the walls covered with current posters and pictures, all serve to remind him of what he stands to lose.

He's steeped in this room. He's aware of a smell he can only describe as the smell of classroom, his classroom. Pictures of his form flitter through his brain. The remembered noise of their clattering resounds in his head as they surge through the door, to scramble to their seats, babbling and exchanging news with their mates.

Shaking the pictures from his brain, he returns to the present. Picking up his box of personal belongings he turns at the door, looks back on his domain before leaving and finally clicking the door behind him.

The anaesthetic wears off and the pain of his thoughts brings a sob to his throat. Never before has he fully realised how much he loves teaching, or what a huge part this school and its life, play in his world. He knows all these kids. He knows their parents and siblings, their aunts, uncles and grandparents.

Who will take his classes, form assemblies, hobbies and study groups? Who will believe the accusations and who support him? How well does one person know another, to the extent of absolute certainty of how they will behave? He thinks wryly he will soon discover who his true friends are.

Cohesive thought is again in full flow and along with it, an emotion he doesn't recognize. What is going to happen to him in the next few days? What should he do? First he must go straight home and ring Rick his solicitor friend. Then await contact from the Police. Again he is seized by this unfamiliar emotion, this consuming passion. Is it fear?

As far as he can remember, he's never really been afraid of anything. He recognizes it now. It's anger. He's dominated by a fury he's never before experienced. He wants to hit out at somebody or something. The alien emotion swamps his reason, making survival and self-defence a primeval need. How could this happen to anybody in this day and age? How could it happen to *him*? How could a chit of a girl cause such havoc in a person's life? An inner voice tells him it is happening more and more these days. It is an occupational and professional hazard and surprisingly is new on his horizon. Kids are so knowing and aware these days.

Letting himself in the front door where stairs climb from the hall to the upper storeys, Tom is greeted by the silence of an empty house, an unusual occurrence. They are either all in or all out and he is usually first away while the calls of 'have you seen my library book' or 'Mum where did you put my trainers?' are still floating from above. It's rare for him to be the first person home.

The emptiness wraps him like a chill mist. Coats hang listlessly from the hall stand, their sleeves sagging emptily, umbrellas stand to attention and boots fight for supremacy in the base tray. Everything is the same as always. Only he is different.

Hearing a faint 'mew' Tom looks upstairs and sees their young kitten staring down at him with eyes wide and unblinking.

"Hello Mitzi. Did I spoil your snooze? Come down here then. Come Mitzi."

The small body bounds towards him and Tom scoops her up and cuddles her furry warmth to his chest and rubs his chin on her head. His anger has dissipated during his brisk walk home but the still house disturbs him further. He needs to share this thing, which has stopped his life. It is so unfair, so unjust and he's ill-equipped to manage it. He wants to tell Hazel, to feel her warmth and understanding. 'Hey!' Will she believe in him, or will she recoil in revulsion? They met at college and have weathered a lot together, but never anything like this.

His wife is a peripatetic teacher of music specialising in flute and violin and visits all the schools up and down the Dale, giving lessons from Tuesday to Friday. On Mondays she says her job description is 'just a housewife.' Tom's first impulse is to ring her and his hand hovers above the phone. The thought of her worrying about him all day and being unable to do anything to help, stops him. Sitting in the kitchen with the kitten curled on his lap he picks up the phone. Rick's secretary answers when it connects to his office and while waiting to speak to him, Tom wonders what his friend's reaction will be. He is soon to learn.

"Hello there Tom, what can I do for you?"

His friend's voice holds a note of surprise.

"Rick I need to see you urgently and professionally. I'm at home. How soon can you fit me in?"

"Oh! Let's see now. I've a free hour at ten-o-clock; I'll call and see you then. Are you all right Tom?"

"No Rick, but I'm not ill. See you at ten."

"Rightho. Get the kettle on lad."

Tom puts the kitten in her basket and switches on the coffee pot. He mooches into the sitting room and prowls around. Lifting a photo of Joe from the shelf, he gazes at it moodily. His son is thirteen and at the end of year nine in the school where Tom teaches. It is the only secondary school in the area except for the Catholic Establishment in Richmond. Tom is proud of the way their son is developing. Joe is a loving, honest boy with a cheerful healthy attitude. What will this do to him when the news hits the town? Replacing the picture, he stares at the photo of his beautiful daughter, a recent picture taken when she finished sixth form. With her dark chestnut curls, her vivid violet eyes and with that smile, she could have the world at her feet.

"Well my lovely girl. What will this do to you? You'll find who are your real friends too I think."

Wendy is going on to university and will be away soon, but what about the next few weeks when she will feel the backlash? How will boyfriend Brad view events and how will he react? At the moment he's trying to persuade Wendy to scrap her plans for university and stay at home. Gentle, soft-hearted Wendy. He feels again the soft, auburn, little girl head nestling into his shoulder, the feel of her small hand trustingly in his. He pictures the misery in those wide eyes, but he can never imagine the hurt and strain this affair is going to inflict upon their previously content and untroubled lives.

"Tom? Where are you?"

Rick's voice interrupts this train of thought and he goes to greet his friend's entrance at the front door, leading him into the kitchen. Rick stands staring at his long time comrade, silently pouring out two mugs of fragrant coffee.

"Tom? What the hell's brought you home at this time of day? What's happened?"

"Come through and sit down while I tell you."

After a short pause while they settle in the sunny front room Tom blurts out,

"I've been accused of child molesting, and I'm suspended."

Rick's mug slams back down on the table with a plop.

"The devil you have."

After an initial shocked exclamation, Richard Halton listens without interruption to the events of the morning, since the two of them parted after their run just a few hours earlier.

"This is Frank Grayson's girl you're talking about? The precocious, blonde piece?"

"The same. She's never any trouble in school but does have problems, of that I'm sure. The biggest of these is her family I should think. I'm expecting the Police to contact me at any time. Will you act on my behalf Rick?"

"Course I will, goes without saying. I must just ask you this Tom. Did you touch this girl?"

"Well yes, I did but not in that way and we were not alone."

Tom relates the incident on the cliff top about which he told the headmaster.

Rick counts on his fingers,

"Now let me get this right. Annette and her companion Melissa Dean were frolicking around at the cliff edge. You saw them, went up between and behind them, put a hand on the shoulder of each and yanked them back. Is this in view of others in the party? Is Melissa Phillip Dean's girl?"

"That's right but I'm not aware that anybody witnessed the incident. They may have. I was too busy chewing them up and reminding the girls of safety rules I'd stressed before we started out."

Rick picks up his mug and sips thoughtfully,

"Are these two girls close friends then, a bit unlikely I should think?"

"Well, not exactly. Annette Grayson doesn't have any really close friends. I think Melissa feels a bit sorry for her so perhaps keeps her company. Melissa's close friend is Mandy Eastwood but she didn't come with us that day. Come to think of it, Annette Grayson spends most of her school breaks with her cousin, Sally Foster in year ten. You remember Maggie Smith, lives over in Windleby? Well she, Annette's mother Wilma Grayson and Sally Foster's mother Chris, are sisters. Their mother has the sweet shop in Waithe."

"Do you think then that this incident on the cliff top is the occasion the girl is referring to and she's misinterpreted the action or embroidered it a bit?"

"Oh hell Rick. Come on. I'm no child molester. She couldn't possibly have thought a grab on the shoulder was a touch-up and that's the one and only time I've laid a finger on her. But--" Tom hesitates prompting Rick to ask,

"But what? Is there something else?"

"Not really it's just that Peter Finch said there is another occasion that Grayson wouldn't tell him about."

"Mmm, I can sympathise with your frustration, but I have to get it straight in my head. You see, until we hear what you're actually being accused of, there isn't much we can do. Why don't you give me a ring when the

Police have been in touch and we'll go from there?"

Richard puts his mug on the table and leaps to his feet.

"Must run, I've a client at 11-o-clock. Keep busy Tom and try not to mope. We'll soon have you out of this mess."

Tom gets up from his seat and looks his friend in the eyes.

"Do you think I did this Rick?"

"I know you didn't. We've been buddies since we shared nappies. You were always more interested in fossils than girls."

"But men my age do strange things they say. Have you no doubts?"

"None at all lad, none at all. Stay in touch now."

Tom had been almost one hundred per cent certain of his friend's belief in him but it's reassuring to have it confirmed and he feels more optimistic after seeing Rick out.

He feels renewed alarm however, when he sees the police car pull up in front of the house.

CHAPTER TWO. THE CHARGE.

The police station is in the High Street and there is usually a sergeant on duty for enquiries but no custodial accommodation. Clients under arrest are taken to Richmond. Tom knows all the lads in the local force and plays cricket with two of them. All three live in the town and their children attend his school. The Inspector shares himself between here and Richmond. It is Inspector Mike Shaw who emerges from the passenger seat and Police Sergeant Will Metcalfe who joins him at the gate. The latter usually plays second bat and is a good spin bowler. Does it feel worse or better that he knows these chaps? Will they believe him? It must be as difficult for them as for him.

He waits until the front bell rings before opening the door to them. The Inspector speaks first,

"Good morning Mr. Prescott, I think you know our errand."

"Yes Inspector. Please come in."

"Morning Tom. This is a bad job for you."

"Good morning Will. Yes, a bit of a shock too."

Tom settles the two officers in the sitting room and pours them coffee.

"Well now Tom,"

Inspector Shaw bowls the first ball,

"I can't keep calling you Mr. Prescott, I've known you too long. When I rang Mr. Finch, he told me he had to suspend you pending enquiries and told us you were at home.

I sympathise with his decision even if it is a little premature. We shall be seeing him later this morning to note his conversation with Mr. Grayson."

The Inspector keeps his eyes on Tom as he takes a swig from his coffee mug.

"That gentleman came to the police station at eight thirty this morning with a very serious complaint. He says his daughter Annette has admitted to him that you committed a serious offence against her. An offence of a sexual nature. Can you explain this?"

Tom again relates the tale of the cliff top at Whitby, while Mike Shaw listens attentively and Will Metcalf scribbles on his note pad. Tom finishes,

"Is this the occasion she means Inspector?"

"No Tom, although Mr Grayson did mention that. When was this outing?"

Reaching for his diary Tom replies,

"I can tell you exactly. It was Friday April 10th."

"The incident he's complaining of is alleged to have occurred last Saturday, the 18th. At around eleven am. to be precise."

Fresh shock waves rip along Tom's electronic system and he can't hide the dismay and horror he feels. Coffee sloshes as his mug hits the side table.

"Where's this supposed to have happened and what did I do?"

"Mr. Grayson alleges that his daughter saw you working in your garden wearing only shorts, khaki ones. You waved to her and she waved back. I believe there's a small group of trees between your gardens, which back on to each other. Is that right?"

"Yes. There's a gate into the copse from our garden, Joe and his friends play in there. There's a gap in the Grayson's hedge where he comes through to his compost heap. It's a bit of no man's land about twenty feet or so wide and stretches along the bottom of most gardens here."

"Well, you're alleged to have entered the copse and spoken to her through this gap. You then entered their garden, put your arms around her, kissed and fondled her. She was wearing a bikini and you removed the upper portion."
In his agitation, Tom leaps from his seat,

"Inspector this is a pack of lies. Except for the incident in Whitby, I've never laid a finger on this girl. Good God. She's younger than my own daughter."

"There's more Tom."

Mike Shaw looks at him steadily for a moment while Tom waits for more mines to explode.

"The girl says her parents were at business and your wife, daughter and son went out in the car that morning. She also states that you have a large brown stain or a mole that extends below your waistline on your right back and a scar along your ribs on the same side."

Tom sits down again, suddenly speechless. He knows now how fish feel when trawled up from their safe haven. The soft voice of Will Metcalf reaches him through the net,

"Is there anything in your diary for that morning Tom? Were your family out?"

When Tom finds the page he reads,

"Tidied garden and cut grass. Hazel, Wendy and Joe to Darlington. Hot and sunny. Beat Northellinton 396 declared. Yes, I remember the day. Hazel was back before the match ended and came up to the ground with Joe to watch the last hour. It was an exciting match."

Will agreed,

"Yes it was a great game. Tom, were you wearing shorts in the garden that day?"

"What? Shorts? Oh yes, I usually do and it was hot."

"Did you go into the copse that morning?"

"No-o, I don't think so. Wait a minute. That's the day I painted the gate."

"What colour was that?"

"Oh nothing fancy, just green Cuprinol that I had in the garage."

Mike Shaw's look is serious,

"It doesn't look good Tom. The girl's bikini bottoms have the full imprint of a hand mark on them. In a green colour."

The Inspector produces some pale blue bikini pants, displaying a distinct left hand mark over the left buttock area. "Does your hand fit this mark?"

"Shouldn't think so for a minute. I have a big hand. That's why they put me behind the wicket. In any case I was wearing rubber gloves because I've that kind of skin that reacts to a lot of chemicals."

Tom lays his hand on the imprint completely covering it. Inspector Shaw comments,

"She's a well-built lass I believe and this is stretchy material. Let me pull it and then see." Tom leaps to his feet again and stands clenching and unclenching his hands.

"Good grief Inspector. What are you trying to do to me? Put me away? I didn't do this. I didn't see the girl that day."

"Tom, I have to look at every aspect of this incident as a sharp lawyer will when the case comes to court."

The explosion this time sends Tom reeling to his chair and turns his voice to a croak. His face blanches beneath the freckles, even more pronounced round his mouth.

"Court? It can't get that far surely? It's all lies. She's fantasising. Can't you make her tell the truth? You're cleverer than her. She's just a girl."

"Rest assured Tom, we shall explore every avenue. We need you to come down to the station to make a formal statement." Mike Shaw puts down his coffee mug and stands up.

"Now I should like to see this gate and the copse, and then look into Grayson's garden if you'll lead the way please."

Tom takes them through the rear door and conservatory, across the patio and down the long garden to the clump of Scots pine trees. Their outline against the summer sky, flat tops sculpted in contrast to the unbroken blue, raises them above the trials of humans. Any other time he would have paused to admire their classic magnificence. He loves those trees. This morning he leads the two policemen to the newly painted, green wooden gate, in the neatly trimmed hedge. Lifting the latch Inspector Shaw passes through on to the rough grass beneath the trees.

"That will be Grayson's hedge then and his compost heap?" the Inspector comments.

Will Metcalf stands at the gap in the hedge looking up at the back of the Grayson house. It's a three storey Victorian building and the windows on the first and second floors look over the gardens.

"What kind of terms are you on with Grayson Tom?"

"We very rarely meet, but if we do, we pass the time of day and that's all. He's not a man I particularly want to converse with."

"Do you keep all this stretch tidy?"

"I do ours and Ginny Carter's next door, but only twice a year when I clip the hedges."

The Inspector walks through the gap and stands looking into the corner of the Grayson garden, where the offence is said to have occurred. Coming back through the gate he bends to pick up a pair of yellow plastic gloves well smeared with green paint.

"These yours Tom?"

"Yes. Those are the ones I was wearing that morning."

"All right if I hang on to them?"

"Of course."

Tom's mind is racing. What a stupid place to leave the bloody gloves. What is Shaw making of it?

Back at the patio Mike Shaw seats himself in a garden chair.

"Tom. Tell me about the gloves. You're a tidy man I should have thought."

"I think I am but Hazel wouldn't agree. The gloves? As usual time was pressing and I was cutting it fine. The match was due to begin at one-o-clock. By the time I'd finished the gate and cleared away the stuff it was eleven thirty. There was a screw loose on one of the hinges so I took off the gloves and was tightening that when the phone rang. It was Matt Cross to say he'd be a few minutes late but not to worry, he'd be there."

"You can hear the phone from down there?"

"Oh yes, there's an extension bell up there above your head." Tom points above the door.

"Did you return to the gate?"

"No and haven't since then. Hence the gloves."

"The screw driver you used will still be in the house?"

"Screwdriver? Can't remember what happened to that. I might have put it in my kitchen drawer being a tidy man, or Hazel may have."

Tom leads the way through the rear entrance, across the conservatory and into the kitchen. Striding over to the drawers beneath a work surface he opens the bottom drawer and pounces on a medium screwdriver as though it were exhibit B.

"That's it, that's the one I used. See the green paint."

"Yes I see. Well now I want you to come down to the station with us and make a formal statement. You understand we're not making any charges at the moment, this is just a preliminary enquiry."

Tom accompanies the two officers to the official Police car and sits in the back. The sensation is of sitting in a fish bowl.

Several people stare as the car passes and more people notice as he alights at the station. He supposes people are interested in whom the police are escorting whatever the reason, but the person is him and he feels as conspicuous as a streaker on a cricket pitch.

He's taken to the interview room where he faces Mike Shaw over a desk. Will Metcalf sits nearby activating a tape recorder.

"Don't worry about this Tom, its routine procedure now. All interviews are recorded for your protection as well as ours."

Inspector Shaw again starts the batting,

"Can you tell me what you remember of your

movements on that Saturday morning Tom?"

"Yes, I think I can do that. Out for a run at six fifteen with Rick Halton. Back and showered around seven, breakfast with Hazel, Wendy and Joe around eight. A quick look at the paper. Things are a bit more relaxed at the weekend.

Hazel put out the washing and Wendy and Joe do their own rooms. The family were off to Darlington before eight thirty and I did the chores, you know filled the dishwasher and tidied round. That takes us to about nine -o - clock."

"And then?"

"I went into town with the shopping list. Eastwood's butchers first, Dave Paxton was away that week but Ron Sharpe was playing fifth bat. Josh Eastwood lets them make up the time in the week. I chatted to them a few minutes and bought meat. From there I went over to the supermarket to pick up one or two provisions, then the bakers and then up to the library. I think it was just after ten when I arrived home."

"You're a quick worker. So between ten and twelve you did the gardening?"
The Inspector's eyes continue probing.

"Yes. I cut the grass, that takes about twenty minutes, tidied the borders a bit then decided to do the gate. The rest you know. How does all this help for heaven's sake?"

"Patience Tom. It helps to form a picture. If we're to help you, we need to know it all. I noticed you're completely screened and private, near the house in your back way and can't see into the Grayson's garden at all. In fact, you can only see their top floor and roof from your patio and lawn. Very nice."

"That's the way we like it."

"Well, I think that's all Tom. We may think of things to ask you later on but that's it for the moment. If you have anything to add, give me a ring or pop in."

Will switches off the tape recorder then walks to the door with Tom. He squeezes his arm as he is leaving,

"Try not to worry lad. Have you talked to Rick?"

"Yes he came first thing. How the hell can I help but worry? My career's on the line here. Whatever the outcome, the damage is already done."

The voice of Inspector Shaw reaches him at the door,

"By the way Tom. What did you do the next day, Sunday?"

This took Tom by surprise; surely Sunday isn't in question.

"We were all at home all day. We had people over for lunch and ate outside on the patio. The Haltons joined us in the afternoon and we had a barbeque around six. Why?"

"I just wondered. You lead a busy life."

Back at home with his thoughts and unaccustomed free time he feels as a man overboard must feel, abandoned, adrift and aimless, trying desperately to keep afloat against an overpowering current. For the first time in his life, he is not in control of his own life. He feels as though he's a puppet being manipulated by another hand and dangling in space. The empty stillness of the house presses in on him, suffocating him, muffling his willpower.

He scrapes his mind for the list of things he's going to do when he finds time. There's the shed to paint, that bit of patio wall to repair, Hazel's sewing machine to overhaul, his cricket pads to scrub and many more tasks awaiting his attention. Firstly because he needs normality and reassurance, he rings Rick and is put through immediately, although he is with a client.

"Hello there, bring me up to date."

"Inspector Shaw and Will Metcalf have visited and I've been down to the station. I can't believe what's happening. I feel steamrollered. I don't know what to do Rick."

"Well to begin with, you can join me for lunch at the 'Sheaf' at one-o-clock, if you've nothing better on the timetable. You can fill me in on the full story then. The worst thing you can do is to hide away. However difficult it is, go out and meet it. You're innocent lad, show 'em. See you at one and I'll have my usual ginger ale."

After replacing the phone, Tom resumes his restless pacing. Twelve fifteen, there's time to put in some work on next year's timetable for year eleven. Halfway to his den the thought strikes him that he might not be in school next term. He could be in prison, serving a sentence for child abuse.

CHAPTER THREE. UPDALE.

In the office of the head of Fossrig school. Hazel Prescott is discussing the progress of her music pupils. The head, Mrs Smith, passes her a sample programme for their annual concert.

"I've put in some work on this Hazel, what do you think? We heads have at last agreed a date, but that depends on your being available. Would May 12th. be a good evening for you? It's the Friday before we break for a week and we would begin at seven o-clock. Haytime will start after that you see and you know everything stops for that. Second cut will be in late July so it has to be between times. It's a job to fix these occasions into the farming calendar for the greatest attendance."

"Oops. That's the last week of the Waithe show but the week after your break would be fine with me." Hazel chuckles as she looks at her diary and says,

"Seeing as the farmers are our most loyal and generous patrons, we have to consider them."

Mrs Smith scribbles in her diary and approves the date,

"Friday 26th will be just right, may be better actually." She pauses with pen poised,

"I'd forgotten the show. What is it you're doing this year?"

"The Merry Widow this year. Some lovely songs but our producer has us chorus girls in fishnets would you believe!"

"He wants a bit of leg then uh? We must book our seats as it's always booked up early. I'm sure it will be terrific as always."

In her gentle voice Hazel continues,

"Could we exchange Bella Foster with Jake Fawcett do you think? If Bella has to wait until the second half to play, she may disintegrate. She's such a nervous little thing just lately. Jake's tough, he can manage the waiting. Yes, everything else appears satisfactory. I may change the piece Raymond's playing, but I'll decide that after today's lesson."

The Head fondles a pendant at her throat.

"Hazel I'm glad you mentioned Bella, I'm a little concerned about her. Will you pay special attention to her please? She seems to be retreating further into her shell. I wondered if she is being bullied but have neither seen nor heard anything, in fact the other children are protective of her rather than the reverse."

"I'll watch her Mrs Smith and give her the chance to tell me if something's troubling her."

Hazel leaves the office and heads for the hall where pupils will come to her for their lesson of fifteen minutes each. Music tuition in school is free, precious and jealously guarded. The Education Department have rumbled for the past few years about imposing a fee and charging parents a set amount each term for children taking lessons or of scrapping it altogether. This move is vigorously opposed and so far has not been introduced here as in other counties.

Dales villages scatter a wide area, children funnelling into the Comprehensive School in Weyburne in their twelfth year. There is a fine youth orchestra, which brings fame to the Department in the several competitions held throughout Yorkshire. The orchestra is fortunate enough to have a leader, made redundant from his post of Musical Director of a large city school, during their severe cutbacks. Nicholas Chaplin is an inspiration, enthusiastic and energetic. He puts the polish on the knowledge and skill the pupils acquire from their lessons and practice, drawing them together as a team with one aim; to give of their best to please him and others. He is also the conductor of the Waithe silver band, the, Waithe Operatic Society, and the Dales Orchestra encouraging children who play in school to continue their musical options.

Although her specialist instruments are flute and violin, Hazel Prescott is versatile and if it's music she can play it. She teaches the basics of the few instruments provided by the Education Department and the many others donated by parents or provided by proceeds from various fund raising events and concerts throughout the villages.

One by one, the pupils take their lesson, playing what they have practised and going over a new piece to work on through the week, giving attention to timing, expression and theory. The last pupil before break is Bella Foster, a pretty, blonde girl in her last year at junior school.

"Hello Bella, come and sit down love. How are you today?"

Hazel's soft gentle voice is interested and her tone warm. The girl sits by her side and takes out her violin and music.

"All right thank you Mrs Prescott."

"Play your piece for me please dear."

The girl looks tired and worried with dark smudges under her lovely blue eyes. She plays her piece on her instrument with a surprising confidence and expertise.

"That's very good Bella. If you play at the concert like you do for me, you'll be a knockout. Is anything worrying you about your piece?"

"No Mrs. Prescott, I like it."

The girl's voice is hesitant and uncertain.

"Do you have a lift to rehearsal on Friday or is that a problem for you?"

Bella looks away, busying herself with putting her music in the folder. The blonde veil of her hair swings forward as she bends down, hiding her face.

"Janet Sumpter's Dad takes a car full from here but there isn't room for me, so I stay at Aunty Wilma's. Mum picks me up on Saturday morning when she comes in for the shopping."

Her voice is tense and tight. Hazel waits with that quality of quiet waiting so special to her. The girl comes back to sit beside her but says nothing more.

"How does Sally manage, does she stay at your aunt's too?

"No, she stays with her friend Mandy Eastwood. Mum picks us both up the next morning."

Together they look through a new sheet of music that Hazel produces, before asking her to try and play it. After Bella makes a good attempt, Hazel rises to stand behind the girl, with her arms around her slender young body. As she corrects Bella's hand on the bow she feels the child relax against her, almost snuggling into her arms. The small hand trembles beneath her own. Her mothering instinct in direct conflict with professional training, Hazel resists the temptation to enfold the girl and contents herself with patting her hand.

"That was a very good try Bella. If you will work on that this week please and we'll look at it again next Tuesday."

The girl holds the music and looks at Hazel nervously for a few moments before putting it inside her folder. The lesson over, she packs away her instrument slowly as though she doesn't want to leave.

"Who is your Aunty Wilma Bella?"

"Wilma Grayson at Grayson's outfitters in Weyburne Mrs Prescott."

Again the child's voice sounds tight and worried, her eyes busy on her fingers.

"So Annette Grayson is your cousin?"

"Yes, I sleep in her room on Fridays."

The girl finishes her task and begins to leave the hall with dragging feet.

"Shall I see you on Friday at rehearsal Mrs. Prescott?"

"You will Bella. By the way, I've put you in to play first at the concert, will you manage that? We need somebody who plays well to start us off."

The girl's wan little face lights up,

"Yes that's fine Mrs Prescott but I don't mind when I play."

"All right dear, I'll see you at the weekend, - and Bella—"

The girl turns to face her, a look of enquiry on her face,

"Yes Mrs Prescott?"

Quietly Hazel says,

"You do know if something is bothering you that you can tell me don't you? It wouldn't be like telling somebody in school and I may be able to help you sort it out. Look love, take this card, it has my home number and you can give me a ring if you think I can help."

The girl takes the card, looks at it and hesitates before stuffing it into her blouse pocket and muttering.

"Thank you Mrs. Prescott."

Watching the sad little figure with drooping shoulders leave the hall, Hazel reflects that she almost had it then.

"What did you think of Bella today Hazel?" Mrs Smith is waiting to ask.

"The child is carrying a load too heavy for her. She's not quite ready to tell me yet but I've left the lines open."

The little yellow mini noses its way on the back road north of the River and further up the Dale. The light on the contours of the hills is achingly sharp this morning, searching out every crater and flaunting brightness on every peak.

'Could there ever be a more beautiful place to live,' muses Hazel as the car bowls up and down the straight, narrow switchback road. The local farmers say that when the hills are clear and close, it will rain inside twenty-four hours. She won't be sorry about that, might clear the air a bit.

The Romans left remains over at Borebridge as well as this long straight road, as proof of their passage. When she and Tom were first married, it was touch and go whether Tom took the post he was offered in Weyburne or the alternative in Birmingham. Although he left the decision to her, she knew his heart was here, in the Dales. She thanks her lucky stars almost every time she drives around the countryside that they came to Weyburne. Even in the bleak adversity of northern winters, there is colour and a harsh beauty. She watches the clouds dancing towards the east, leaving splodges of moving shade on the hillside.

Smiling, she thinks of all the times farmers helped rescue her and the Mini in bad road conditions. Tucked in the boot along with her musical requirements, is a gallon can of petrol, a rope, a yellow rain jacket and a lamp. These necessities are supplemented in winter with a box of ashes, a shovel and a piece of old carpet. The car tyres suffer several punctures but with practice she is now adept at changing a wheel. However it wouldn't be long before a tractor rumbled by and a driver jumped out with a

"Now lass, you got a problem? Soon fix that for you."

Man of few words is the Dalesman. They are such a lucky family to live here. Too lucky?

Don Travers, Headmaster of Waithe School welcomes the music teacher with his usual cheeky grin, as she enters their staff room.

"Hello there Hazel. When are you coming to work for us full time then? Is it this week or next?

"Neither, I'm afraid. Not until you can pay my salary. What would I teach anyway, the only thing I know anything about is music."

"And people my dear." He wags his finger at her.

"Our children tell you things we don't know. I'm the big bad wolf around here and you're the shining angel it seems."

Don Travers gets up and puts some papers onto his desk. Then picking up a long setsquare and holding it as a cricket bat says,

"Tom played a good game again on Saturday. He hit four sixes one after the other. Great stuff. They shouldn't stuff him behind the wicket, he's a good batsman."

"Yes, wasn't it an exciting game, he was well pleased with everybody. I was there to see some of it, but missed most of the game the previous week."

"Tut tut. A wife's proper place on a summer Saturday afternoon, is watching her husband play cricket, making cucumber sandwiches for the Vicar and serving teas. Remember that."

He swipes a screwed up piece of paper with his set square and twinkles at Hazel.

"You're in the corner of the hall today m'dear, but it's better than your usual squat in the cloakroom. Watch out for Marie Smith, she's a bit fragile today. Her Gran just died this morning. You knew Mrs Sumpter who had the sweet shop?"

"Oh goodness. Yes, I have a sweet tooth and I've often been in there. What a terrible shock, I am sorry."

The Upper Dales School is hopelessly inadequate for the number of pupils coming in from outlying farmsteads and hamlets, plus the offspring of the growing township. There are two outside Porta-cabins to house the upper classes and two classes in the hall, in addition to the overcrowded reception class.

There are five junior Dales schools with Waithe at the head. Four on the south side of the river, each built originally to accommodate children until their education was complete. Now they are inadequate to house ages five to eleven, when the pupils move on to Weyburne Comprehensive.

The fact that children funnel into one senior school provides a common purpose to parents and relatives up and down the Dale, uniting them for or against any new policy. Practically all local people have relatives or in-laws in different villages. Hazel knows the policy of the three wise monkeys, see all, hear all and say nowt, is the only rule by which to live in this locality.

She has worked hard to develop her gift of quiet stillness, which gives children and adults the confidence to share their troubles. A counselling degree gives her the required skills to help them talk, identify the cause of their problem and decide what they can do about it. She feels humbled and privileged in her position. People trust her; they know she will never betray their trust.

Screened away in a corner of the hall with the working hum of two classes buzzing around her, Hazel listens to her pupils. They love to come to her and usually have some little titbit to tell of what is happening in their lives. Today it is Marie's Gran, Mrs Sumpter dying, which is to the fore. They don't know why she died but who will keep the sweet shop now and what will Marie do?

When it's Marie's lesson, the little tear stained face touches Hazel's soft heart and she cuddles the child.

"Try and remember the good things you shared love, some people never knew their Gran, but you had some lovely times with yours didn't you?"

"Yes, she was funny and made me laugh. Did you have a Gran Mrs Prescott?"

"Everybody has two dear, but one of mine died before I was born and the other when I was so tiny, I don't remember her. You know, you'll have to help your Granddad because he'll miss her such a lot. That could be your special job couldn't it?"

"You mean keep him company?"

"Yes, that's right love and bake him little treats like you and your Gran used to do. Now play me your piece please."

Hazel brings sandwiches for lunch, which she eats in the staff room when she's 'Updale' as it is called.

"Dry crust and hard cheese again Hazel. You know you can always have lunch with us."

"Yes I do know that Don and thank you, but I never feel like a meal at midday. Perhaps in the winter I'll take you up on your offer."

"Hmm. How was Marie? Tearful?"

"Yes she was. I should tell you I gave her a cuddle, she is so heartbroken."

"That's OK. I think most of us did. It was such a shock. It happened around eight thirty apparently."

"This morning you mean? I wondered why Fossrigg hadn't mentioned it when I was there. Isn't Marie cousin to Bella Foster?"

"That's right, but Sally and Bella would have left for school you see and nobody could believe she was dead until Dr. Horner saw her."

"You don't know any reason why little Bella Foster should be desperately unhappy do you Don?"

"Ooh. Can't say I do, but I should think having Frank Grayson for an Uncle is enough to make a saint miserable wouldn't you? He's a creep."

"Ye-es, perhaps you're right. That's Tom's opinion of him too. How are your lifts to rehearsal arranged on Fridays? Would anybody have room for Bella? There's a car full already from Fossrig so she apparently stays overnight at Grayson's."

"I should think Bill Royston could fit her in, there's only Malcolm and Heather Stead in his car. She doesn't play a tuber or anything like that does she?"

Hazel laughs,

"No just a violin. Maybe the child will be happier if she can get home after rehearsals. I can't have her unhappiness spoiling her playing. That child's a natural. Will you see if you can arrange it Don?"

"Leave it with me Hazel and I'll see what I can do."

When Hazel drives through the throbbing little town of Waithe, the market is in full swing on the cobbles in front of the pubs in the High Street. It's early April and a lovely sunny day as the smell of fruit and vegetables mixed with leather, sheep and cows, seeps in through the open car window. People are milling around in print dresses and short-sleeved shirts, standing in groups chatting or slipping busily between stalls.

Opposite the market stalls are the stores selling provisions, the chemist and the bakers alongside clothing shops. After the chippie stands the Market Hall, where Hazel attends rehearsals for the 'Merry Widow' on Wednesday evenings . The hall hosts auction sales on a regular basis. This generates cash for local causes like Playshool, Brownies and Cubscouts, by letting out the refreshment room. The sales also provide a source of great enjoyment because of the very varied clientele and the items for sale. These are often tools and things from a bygone age and cause great wonder and fun. The very popular book shop stands nearby.

Vehicles struggle to negotiate the narrow main street without hitting the tourists. The busy little market town hosts large numbers of visitors in the season. People love its rustic charm and hospitable local people. However, they do appear to think that because they are on holiday, everybody else is and the rules of the road don't apply to them. They saunter from side to side in their brightly coloured shorts and shirts regardless of traffic, like puppies off the leash. The scene is so normal, so ordinary yet special to Waithe. The market has been in existence for hundreds of years and except for dress and merchandise, is probably little changed. The same family names are here now as then and the main street is practically unchanged. The shops are unique. Many are family run businesses and very different from the usual high street stores in bigger towns. Hazel noses carefully through the throng and up the winding road on the south side of the river to her next destination.

Borebridge is her last school today and Hazel steers the Mini into the car park by the river. Today the water is low and smells like a drain. They need some rain after weeks of dry windy weather. There is still a good channel of water trickling languidly along the bedrock river bottom, but she longs to see the impatient rush that carries the little river down to the Ure after rain. The past month has been the driest anybody can remember at a time when the rainfall should have been high.

Sitting the mini in the one reaming space, Hazel hops out and takes out her gear. Being a few minutes early she walks to the side of the building and gazes out over at the vista that opens before her eyes. The hills and fields with sheep and cattle contentedly grazing or ambling through the sultry day. The scene is enchanting and very photogenic.

"The mood of people is so very sensitive to weather," she muses, collecting her things.

"Perhaps emotions are affected by air pressure and tend to boil over if a storm threatens."

Hazel is aware that her mood is highly sensitive today, as though the storm clouds are gathering.

CHAPTER FOUR. COUNCIL OF WAR

The last music pupil is timed for three-o-clock in Borebridge and this just gives Hazel time to be home for Joe who leaves at three forty five. It takes between fifteen and twenty minutes to travel the distance between Borebridge and home, depending on obstacles.

These could be caravans, which always travel in two's and three's, farm machinery, school buses and cows going in or out of the farms for milking. It is a novelty to the tourist to see the straggling herds, for among them are often one or two lambs and goats arguing with the accompanying collie and maybe even some hens and a cock to complete the pastoral scene.

Local people know a way can be forged through the huge placid beasts and the contingency of flies that are camp followers. Holidaymakers don't know this and probably cope with motorway traffic at peak times, far better. They and those behind them, can be held in a queue for ten minutes or more, until the field gate or farmyard is reached and the plodding, udder swinging cows turn off the road..

Joe is walking homewards with his pals as the yellow mini passes and Hazel waves but continues on up the hill to turn in the drive to No 8, Mooredge. Easing herself and her paraphernalia from the drivers seat, she looks up to see Tom emerging from the house door.

"Hello love, you're home early. Anything wrong?"

"Yes. I have to tell you before Joe comes."

Hugging her to him, he mutters,

"I needed your calm sense badly today. Sit down here."

He sits on a kitchen stool, pulling her onto the one beside him. There she listens carefully while he briefly relates the events of the day. Jumping up, she hugs him in her arms.

"Oh, my dear, this is a terrible thing to happen to anybody, but to you of all people."

Joe enters the kitchen to see his Mum's arms wrapped around his Dad and his head on her chest.

"Dad? Mum?"

Dropping his satchel, Joe stands uncertainly in the middle of the floor until Hazel stretches out an arm to include him too.

"Dad, why do you have to stay away from school? Mr. Finch says you wouldn't be teaching while some investigations were under way."

"That's right Joe. Wait until Wendy comes home and I'll tell you about it; she and Amy are in Northellerton today at the library. They'll be home for tea."

Hazel adds,

"You know we always hold a council meeting when there's something to discuss. Well this time it will be a council of war. Are you doing your homework now or later? Now? Off you go then while I whip up a Spanish pancake and salad for tea. I'll give you a shout when it's ready."

Tom prepares the salad and Hazel clears the fridge of bits and pieces, leftovers and eggs. She pours oil into a large pan and slices and fries an onion, bacon and potatoes. Spreading the chopped mixture into a deep tin with the left over peas, beans, grated cheese, tomatoes, mushrooms, herbs and whisked eggs, she places it in the hot oven.

During these culinary preparations, they discuss the visit of Inspector Shaw and Will Metcalfe. With the smell of frying onions and parsley floating in the air, Tom turns to Hazel, kitchen knife in one hand and fork in the other.

"Do you think I did this Hazel?"

"Of course I don't, you chump." Flapping the oven cloth at him, "I know you didn't."

"But how do you know? You were out. I was alone here."

Putting her arms around his middle she says simply,

"I know you, my squeaky clean man. I would know if you have any quirky leanings."

Tom said sadly into her hair,

"But there will be people who believe it and some who aren't sure."

"We'll deal with that when it happens. Tom, we all believe in you and so will your friends. You've lived here all of your life and people know you better than you think."

Wendy's friend Amy Hargill stays for tea and hears the story Tom has to tell, ending with,

"I want you all to be quite sure without any doubts that there is no truth whatsoever in these allegations. Wendy, do you have anything you want to say?"

"Yes Dad, I do. I certainly don't believe a word of it, in my book you're the best Dad in the world."

"Thank you Wendy. Amy, any comments?"

"Yes Mr. Prescott. I think you're true blue as well. But what worries me is, if this isn't true and we know it isn't; this girl has made it all up like a fairy tale and told somebody, maybe to get attention. I think that's pathetic."

"Yes Amy you're right, I hadn't thought that far. Why did she need to do it? I wonder. What about you Joe?"

"Well, I think it's a load of crap, er, sorry Dad rubbish. Most of the kids in our year are on your side, although nobody knows what it's all about."

Joe shovels a heaped forkful of omelette into his mouth and mumbles,

"Mr.Finch just said you would be away while some investigations are completed."

Hazel says quietly,

"I think you all should be aware, that people will be taking sides and you may come up against unpleasantness and nasty remarks. We should be seen out and about together as often as possible to show there are no breaks in the ranks. Don't try to protect each other and keep things to yourselves. If something unpleasant happens, tell us about it so we can share it. That way we can weather the storm."

"Will you have to go to court Dad?" Joe sounds quite excited about this sudden thought. He's never been to court.

"Well, if the matter isn't cleared up in a few days and the police think there's a case, then I may have to go before the magistrates to answer an allegation of child molesting. I hope it doesn't come to that, because mud clings and splashes over everybody. We shall meet that possibility if it happens. Now, any other business?"

Wendy clears her throat and looks uncomfortable. Tom grins at her and says,

"Come on what's on your mind?"

"Well Dad, changing the subject. I've been thinking, I may decide to go to college instead of Uni. I could do social sciences or management. I wouldn't need to leave home then."

"Mmm. This sounds like Brad talking. You must do what you want to do Wendy and now's the time to do it, not when you're married with children. Mum and I can only guide you from years of experience. You have a good academic brain that should be trained and Uni is the place for that. If Brad has your interests at heart and wants the best for you, he'll be patient and wait. For God's sake don't think of social work. They carry the can for everybody's inadequacies."

"I just thought it would do no harm to go to Darlington and have a look what's on offer at the college."

A tap on the back door puts an end to this conversation. A small, neat bird of a woman hops into the kitchen. With her red sweater and determined stance she's like an aggressive robin.

"Hello there Ginny, come into our council chamber. We're discussing the events of the day."

"I'm sorry to interrupt your meal. I thought you may have finished."

Hazel seats the little woman in their midst. She looks like an aggressive robin with her red jersey and little pointed nose.

"Don't worry Ginny, we've finished eating. Have a coffee with us, it's ready."

Ginny Carter lives alone next door, under roof with them in the pair of large old semi-detached houses. She lived in that house as a girl, married and raised a family there, as well as caring for elderly parents. She knew Tom's parents, watched him grow up in the town and then welcomed him as a young bridegroom to be her neighbour twenty years earlier.

"Now Tom. What's all this I heard in the town today? They say you were taken to the Police station this morning in their car. Everybody's buzzing with it. Where's my little Kitty puss?" Ginny bends and picks up the kitten before continuing her tirade. "What's going on? What's the real story?"

Hazel pours them all coffee then sits by Tom with her hand on his arm as he once again relates his tale.

Ginny fiercely defends her territory,

"What a lot of garbage, I never heard such rubbish. You say that Head Master suspended you? That's what comes of giving the post to an off cumden! They should have appointed somebody local."

"He was in a difficult position Ginny and has to think of the situation from all sides. He had no choice really but to suspend me."

"Poppycock. That Frank Grayson's another one from Bradford or Wakefield or somewhere like that. They think they can come here with their city ways and fancy ideas and run our lives." Ginny is on her hobbyhorse and goes for the throat.

"I'll never understand why Wilma Sumpter married that Grayson when she could have had a local chap. What does your mother have to say Tom? Bet she's got her battledress on."

"You're right there."

Tom and Hazel exchange an amused glance.

"Feathers all ruffled because somebody attacked one of her chicks. She'll be here any minute. I rang her at lunchtime. It's her bridge club this afternoon."

Hazel's soft voice asks,

"More coffee Ginny? Anyone? Why don't we move into the sitting room, it's still warm from the sun and there are more seats."

While they are trooping from the kitchen and spreading themselves around the spacious, comfortable room, the front door opens to admit a tall silver haired lady. Tom's mother is elegant, tastefully dressed in stylish clothes of timeless fashion. The smooth brow and cheeks give a hint of earlier beauty and even now at almost seventy, Isabel Prescott attracts a second look.

"Well, how things do get around in this town." Isabel flings her coat and bag onto a chair,

"I suppose it will be worse before it's better. Hello Ginny, nice to see you" Isabel leans over to scratch the kitten behind the ear. "you've fallen under her charms I see. Think I know where your vote will be."

Hello my dear." Isabel kisses Hazel on the cheek and hugs Wendy, Joe and Amy.

"Any developments Tom?"

"Not so far Mum. As you know, I had lunch at "The Sheaf" with Rick. Mike Shaw saw him this morning after he and Will were here, but they didn't give anything away. We just have to wait and see."

"Well I've a good mind to go round there and give that little madam a talking to. Making up stories to get folk suspended."
Isabel's cheeks are an indignant pink as she plops into a chair.

"She shouldn't know about such things and *her* only just out of ankle socks. I expect she reads that trash they print in magazines and watches that soap rubbish. I don't know what the world's coming to."

Smoothing her skirts like a ruffled pigeon, Isabel faces the court.

Ginny Carter joins in the defence, she wants to be doing something about it too,

"Why don't you have it out with that Grayson chap and find the truth Tom?"

"I can't do that Ginny. It's a police matter and we have to trust them to sort it out."

The telephone shrills and they all sit to attention, their minds racing to the possible identity of the caller. Tom goes into the hall to answer.

His stomach churns.

"Tom Prescott speaking."

"Hello Tom, I hope you're keeping busy. I'm sorry if I've disturbed your evening meal. I've been in touch with all the members of the Board of Governors and a meeting is arranged for four o-clock tomorrow. The Chairman has requested your presence."

Tom replaces the receiver and purses his lips as he muses,

"Now what's Chairman Rev. Taylor up to? Surely it's out of order for the accused to be present while his fate is discussed?"

CHAPTER FIVE. FOR AND AGAINST.

Because he is cooling his heels at home, Tom wins the chores of shopping and cooking tea. Armed with his list, he takes his courage in both hands and walks into the town the next morning.

He and Hazel share out their custom between stores and he walks into Brumpton's. Ralph Brumpton moved up from Leeds and bought one of the two butchers businesses. He is a bustling, self-important chap as some men who lack inches often are. He stands as second reserve in the cricket team and joins in most social activities in the town.

Unfortunately, the only other customer in the shop at the time is Wilma Grayson, Annette's mother. Tom's cheerful

'Good morning Mrs. Grayson' forces a mumbled response from that lady but a bigger one from Ralph Brumpton. Folding his arms across his chest, he looks Tom in the eye saying,

"I'm afraid I can't serve you today Tom. It isn't that I believe or disbelieve the story, it's just a matter of principle. Until this matter is cleared up, I would rather you didn't come into the shop."

However unprepared he is for this attack, Tom tries not to display his shock. Returning Ralph's look, he says quietly and firmly,

"I'm sorry you feel that way Mr. Brumpton but if you can't serve me today, I feel

I shall be unable to embarrass you with my custom at any time in the future. Good morning and to you Mrs Grayson."

Tom's distress shows in his white, tense face, but his head is high as he steps out of the shop and walks around to High Street and the other butcher. Eastwoods is a long established local firm, employing only family and people in the area. Their attitude is very different. Josh Eastwood comes into the shop from the back and grabs Tom's hand. His dazzling white apron embraces his lean form like a snowdrift and his directness warms Tom.

"Good to see you out lad, I'm blessed if I would have the courage to get out of bed even. You do right to get out there and show 'em you've nothing to hide. Margaret said she'd seen you go into the Police Station yesterday, they haven't charged you have they?"

"No Josh, I had to make a formal statement."

One of the girls serving behind the counter had been his pupil in school and two of the chaps were cricket team-mates. They group around him now, loud in their disgust at his predicament and their support for him.

"They shouldn't have put you out of school Tom. I just cannot believe this could happen here."

"Not to you of all people."

"They'll soon have it sorted lad, don't you worry."

"Just keep your pecker up and show 'em."

Feeling comforted by the kindly faces around him, Tom makes his purchases.

"Thank you all for your support, I'm grateful. I thought everybody would be against me."

"Go on. Nobody with any sense in their heads who knows you, would believe such rubbish."

"See you Thursday night at the meeting. Half seven is it?"

His step lighter and his face brighter, Tom leaves the shop, continues into the market place and enters the baker's shop. Here his reception is the same except for one female customer. As he enters the shop, she leaves it without being served.

"It seems I've lost you a customer Denis, but you don't have to serve me if you'd rather not."

"What, and lose another bloody customer. Don't be daft lad. I've known you since you wore short pants and anything I can help you with, you just let me know."

Encouraged again, Tom buys a crusty brown cob and some pasties. He crosses the market place and steps on to the pavement. Smiling at two town ladies, he says brightly,

"Good morning, lovely day."

One turns her grey head away, the other stares straight through him with hostile eyes, but neither answers his greeting. Tom is shaken by this direct snub, by being judged and found guilty before having a chance to defend himself. If he'd been asked about his position in the little town, Tom would have thought people were with him. He wouldn't have believed there were people ready to think the worst of him by making up their minds from gossip.

He is relieved and very thoughtful on reaching home and realizes it will take a lot of courage to repeat the exercise. Suddenly he feels very tired, as tired as though he'd done eight hours overtime. Hazel rings from school as he's making coffee.

"How was your trip into town love?"

"Traumatic and full of surprises, I hadn't realized there would be such hostility from unexpected quarters. I don't know where the gossip originates and I'm amazed at the speed it travels round this town."

"It's all round the Dale too and people are in two camps. Most of them are for you Tom and send you their support. I'm sorry you had a rough morning. I must go."

"What time will you be home?

"I'll pop in at lunch time for a quick sandwich on my way to Tamthorne. See you then."

Suddenly the big homely kitchen, the busy centre of their family life is too cramped. The baskets of drying herbs, flowers and seed heads, hanging from the old-fashioned clothes rails above the Aga, are closing in around him. He takes his coffee and drags his feet into the sitting room staring dejectedly through the window, but not seeing the sprays of orange blossom or the brilliant flowers rampant in their bid to fulfil their cycle in the neat front garden.

A truck laden with crates of milk bottles, pulls up at the gate and a tall figure of rugby fullback proportions, leaps from the cab and up the path. Here is one chap he knows he can rely on. Matthew Cross, Rick and himself are the same age and attended school together. When Rick and he went on to university, Matt attended Bishop Burton agricultural college. It was expected of him that he help run his father's farm and now because of his parent's poor health, Matt has taken over the reins if not the purse strings. In addition to caring for his large herd of Friesian cows, there is the bottling plant and milk round, covering most of the town and one of the supermarkets.

Reaching the door at the same time, Matt almost falls inside as it opens under his hand.

"Hi there Matt, good to see you. Time for a coffee?"

"Now old mate. What the hell's going on eh? Yes, just a quick coffee thanks. Taken me twice as long to get round this morning. Everybody's buzzing with the news about you and your exploiits. I told them all what I tell you. It's a load of bullshit." Mitzy winds around his legs and he bends to lift her. Holding her up to his face he grins and says

"Wow. You fell in your paws little one. You've grown as much again. Is this the kitten from our place? Nearly as big as her mother." He replaces the kitten on the floor and continues his questioning.

"How did all this start? I can't believe that highhanded, jumped up Finch suspended you and off his own bat too. As a governor, I shall have something to say about that at the meeting."

"Frank Grayson made the complaint at Finch's house on Monday night, so there was no time to consult governors. He had to make an instant decision and act on it. He really didn't have a choice Matt. Thanks for your loyalty, it means a lot to me today."

Tom relates his experiences in the town and his friend erupts like a bottle of fizzy pop.

"Well, from now on my custom goes to someone we can rely on. I don't know, you stick together when you're in business to spread your patronage, but no more. Brumpton'll get his comeuppance, don't you worry." Matt wags a stubby finger in Tom's face and states,

"You know mate, you're going to split this town in two. You realize that? It'll be a long time before the wounds heal."

"You can say that again Matt. I still can't believe this is happening to me."

The discussion continues before veering off to the cricket meeting next evening. This will be held in the back room of the 'Wheatsheaf' Hotel.

"Do you think there'll be any problems with my being on the committee Matt? I'm not sure of Phillip Dean. You know he's been trying to make our meetings more formal and change the venue to the pavilion."

"Yeah!' another bloomin city pratt. They come here thinking they know it all and try to change us when we are all rubbing along quite happily in our own way."

"Lots of folk from school and elsewhere have rung to console and support me, but nothing from him. We have a squash match on

Friday so perhaps he'll have something to say then. He wants the Deputy Head's post when Dick Blendell retires and may think this is a chance to put me out of the running."

"Is that so? I know he has some uppity ideas. I thought at the AGM he's a bad choice for chairman, but nobody wanted the post. Trouble is, we're all too apathetic. We let these incomdens walk all over us, then moan when they want to bring in their city ways."
Matthew drains his mug and pushing it on the table, rises hurriedly to his feet.

"Stop anticipating trouble chum. There shouldn't be any problems. Hey, look at the time. I'll see you at the meeting. Keep smiling mate. Show 'em what you're made of."

Slapping his friend on the shoulder, Matthew makes a hurried exit and the sound of his ancient Ford pick-up roaring away down the road, splits the silence of the area like a rocket in a desert.

Smiling to himself, Tom concludes that the exhaust has blown again. Along with punctures, this is a regular occurrence, as the truck bounces at speed over rocks and bumps in rough farm tracks. He feels warmed and cheered by the visit of his lifelong friend. He'd never doubted Matt's loyalty, but to take time out of his hectic schedule to call in and demonstrate that loyalty is a great comfort.

Hazel's flying visit at lunchtime also helps to keep up his spirits. He describes his jaunt into town and the reaction of people he met. Her eyes on his face, she gives him her full attention.

"What were your feelings in Brumptons?"

"Initially it was shock. I couldn't believe I'd heard correctly. Then I think it was anger and disgust maybe. Pride too. I musn't let them see I was hurt, even if I did feel like a worm sliding out of the shop."

Tom takes out the carton of fruit juice from the fridge and considers his next statement.

"When I thought it over later, I realized he probably wouldn't have said anything if Wilma Grayson hadn't been there. He wants planning permission for an extension at the rear of his shop and needs Grayson's good will, because their properties adjoin. Strange thing about Wilma. I was watching her and she looked more uncomfortable than I felt. Kind of

113

ashamed. Why would she look ashamed Hazel?"

"I don't know love unless she doesn't support him or his charge."

Tom puts the plate of sandwiches he's prepared for their lunch onto the table with tomatoes and crisps while Hazel pours the fruit juice. She motions with the carton,

"Mmm. You could be right about the planning. Poor Wilma, I expect it would be awkward if she was seen to be friendly with you and I've always thought she is frightened of that husband of hers. But what about the Misses Stott? How did that make you feel?"

"Now that did shake me, because they are Dales people. They looked just the same when I was a lad but they've always been odd. You know, I seem to remember they're related to

Wilma Grayson. Sisters to old Mrs Sumpter who just died."

"I didn't know that. Well that could explain their attitude; although I'm sure poor Mrs Sumpter would have acted differently. Tom, you know this whole thing could seriously damage good relations in the town. Local people have welcomed incomers up to now, especially business people, because of the prosperity and variety they bring. This could severely harm all that tolerance."

"Yes, I'm afraid you're right. Matt called in and he said something along the same lines."

CHAPTER SIX. SUPPORT.

Tom stands shoulders slumped, hands deep in pockets, his whole appearance indicating failure and dejection. Hazel watches the tortured expression on his beloved face, once so carefree. The dark russet tint of the hair inherited by Wendy, the fair skin and rugged outdoor look, a give away to his lifestyle. She sees the brooding look in the odd eyes Wendy and Joe find so comic. This episode has come as a seismic shock to him, blitzing his life, bursting the bubble of his innocence and trust.

Growing up in a town like this, in the days before people from outside moved in to live, was like being part of a large family. His younger sister Sarah didn't return to the town after graduating, preferring city life, as did so many of their generation. What is there here for them? Housing is too expensive, there is little work and there is so much more going on in the big world for young people. Sarah qualified as a bio-chemist and landed a top job with a pharmaceutical firm in Calgary, Canada and she is unlikely to return.

Pulling her thoughts back to Tom and his problems, Hazel asks,

"What are you going to do with yourself this afternoon love? Anything planned?"

"I think I shall take myself off for a hike up on the moors. Take the camera. No risk of being snubbed up there."

"Tom love. Next week at this time this will all be behind you like a bad dream. Try to think of it as an episode, a learning experience, role play. Don't take it to heart."

"How can I do that when I feel like the bloody sacrificial lamb? Would you be able to think of it like an exercise if it were happening to you? This is real Hazel. It's happening and it's happening to me."

Hazel gives him a big hug,

"Yes they were careless words Tom. I can't even begin to imagine how you must be feeling. You're missing your school life and the action, it's always been such a big part of your world and now you feel as though you're on the scrap heap or worse."

"Mmm. You've just about hit it there. I never before realised how much of me depends on that place and those kids. It isn't only them who benefit as pupils, but we learn such a lot from them too. They're our future and it gives me such a thrill to think I'm privileged to influence them and teach them what I know. Not just facts, but ethics and principles, caring, living together as citizens and even manners. It's breaking me up Hazel."

"I can understand all of that and feel for you. Oops, I must get a move on. Go off and have a walk sweetheart, it's a lovely day. Take a flask and a bite. I'll see you at tea."

It is most unlike Tom to snap, especially at her. This is really getting to him. Leaving him to make his flask, Hazel speeds off in the mini to her next session in Tamthorne school. Here the Head Miss Polly Baxter is music trained and her influence promotes a strong musical interest among the staff, pupils and parents. Hazel's pupils here will use up a whole afternoon.

She wonders as the mini covers the few miles, whether the news has reached here yet and how Polly has reacted to it. News travels fast on the Dales Network. Once when she bumped the mini Updale in Waithe, Tom knew about it before she arrived home.

She isn't kept long in ignorance. The tall lean figure of Miss Baxter meets her at the door. Dressed in a classic grey suit and white blouse, she looks rigged for the part of a school marm, with her severe hairstyle and prim appearance. Hazel knows this is an act. In reality, Polly Baxter is a hoot. She has a terrific sense of humour, is scrupulously fair, hardworking and inventive.

"Come into the Staff room a moment Hazel."

Two more full time female teachers and one part time elderly assistant are collecting their belongings ready for the afternoon.

"You will forgive us discussing this business about Tom in your absence please Hazel. I am acting as spokesman for all of us here, when I say without reservation, that none of us believe a word of it. I'll bet you anything you like, that this minx has imagined the whole thing and then let it slip out. Whatever, you can assure him of our belief in him and we expect him here as usual on Thursday after school, for cricket practice. Suspended indeed. Well, he's not suspended from this school."

A few parents are standing at the gate waiting to meet infants, when Hazel leaves the school and most of them she knows and acknowledges. Is she imagining pitying looks from others? Certainly, she feels no hostility. Tom will be encouraged when she tells him. Glancing at the petrol gauge and seeing the needle on reserve, she turns into the garage on her way home.

"Fill her up Hazel?"

"Yes please Bruce and will you book it for me?"

"Sure thing. What the devil's your Tom been up to then? Not true is it?"

"No Bruce it's not true, but it will be very hard for him to live down."

"Don't you worry Hazel. We'll see him through. I'll be at the meeting Thursday night."

Bruce plays ninth bat and is an excellent fielder. The committee meeting on Thursday evenings becomes an open cricket club forum, when the business is completed. Players and club members can raise any issues and use it as an excuse for a night out. Hazel thinks it might be quite a lively meeting. It will take Tom out of himself a bit. There is no doubt he is missing his colleagues and busy teaching schedule.

After signing for the petrol Hazel sits rigidly as the thought hits her that she has never considered whether this could all be true and Tom did actually do it. Could he? She feels herself hugging him and knows how good that feels and how spontaneously it happens. How ridiculous to even think it could be true. She has no doubts. Her trust in him is complete. Starting the car she drives home to her family.

CHAPTER SEVEN. THE BOARD.

It is exactly five minutes to four on Wednesday when there is a knock at the door of the Headmaster's study. At the invitation of Peter Finch the tall figure of Tom Prescott enters the room. The Head is shocked by Tom's appearance. The man looks haggard and much older than the last time they met. His face is gaunt and his eyes tired and devoid of their usual sparkle. It is almost as though his inner radiance is reduced to a candle glow, his enthusiasm for life dulled. Good heavens was it only yesterday that he had sent Tom away?

"Ah, good afternoon Tom. Come in. I believe most of the Governors have arrived and if you're ready, we'll join them. No more developments I suppose?"

"No Sir, none. What will happen today?"

"I'm not sure. It's my guess some of them may want you reinstated, but there will need to be agreement on that, probably a vote. Is there anything you wish to ask or say to me before we go in?"

"No Sir, I don't think so. I've nothing to hide and suggest we play it by ear."

The eight governors are seated around the table in the hall when Tom enters with his headmaster. Their conversation stops as the two reach the table and take their seats, Tom to the left of Peter Finch at the opposite end to the chairman.

The Reverend Taylor begins,

"Good afternoon Ladies and Gentlemen. As Chairman of the Board of Governors of Weybury Comprehensive School, I declare this extra-ordinary meeting open. The first and only item on our agenda is the suspension of our Senior Master Tom Prescott. I hasten to add that this was an emergency decision, taken by the Headmaster Mr. Finch in view of the seriousness of certain allegations made against Mr. Prescott. Mr. Finch will you please fill us in with the details, for the benefit of anybody who doesn't already know them."

Peter Finch is feeling uncomfortable and outnumbered. For the first time he questions the wisdom of his decision to put Tom Prescott out of school. He looks around the table and sees that most gathered there are friends or associates of Tom's and he as Headmaster, would probably find himself in the role of defendant. He notes Matthew Cross, Richard Halton, Mrs Beales, Joshua Eastwood and their school secretary Jenny Cloughton, in particular are all gazing at him enquiringly. Well he acted in the best interests of the school. His school.

Briefly he outlines the events leading up to his decision, the fact that Grayson came to his house at 9 o-clock on Monday evening, that he called Tom in to school early on Tuesday morning and called this meeting as soon as it could be arranged.

"I apologize Ladies and Gentlemen if that is out of order but the decision I took was in the best interests of everybody concerned at that time."

He expects a volley from Matthew Cross and is not disappointed.

"Mr. Finch, undoubtedly you considered the best interests of the school at the time of your lone verdict and I don't doubt your sincerity. However, in the light of Tom

Prescott's long and loyal service in this school together with his unblemished record, I question the necessity to suspend him, bearing in mind it was not a unanimous decision of the Governors."

One by one they have their say, opinions flying across the table like ping pong balls. After debating the matter for ten minutes, the Chairman asks,

"Mr. Prescott, I would like to ask if you will return to your post immediately if the opportunity arises?"

"Do you mean before the Police enquiry is complete Sir?"

"It would be with the approval of this Board but prior to the Police enquiry being complete. What would be your answer?"

"Can we see first, whether that approval is forthcoming?"

"Indeed we can. Ladies and Gentlemen, the question is, should Tom be reinstated before Police investigations have cleared him or should we await their verdict. May I please have a show of hands on this?"

Peter Finch thought he should abstain in order to defend his decision but he is not surprised to see the hands of both Matthew Cross and Richard Halton raise instantly, closely followed by Mary Beales. There is a moment's thoughtful pause before the hands of the rest of members are raised.

Counting with his pencil, the Reverend Taylor announces,

"Apart from Mr. Finch and myself as abstainers, the vote is unanimous."

He beams at Tom,

"What do you say Mr. Prescott, do you wish to return to school now?"

"Well Sir, I've been thinking while you all decided my fate and I've decided not to take up your offer. I do appreciate the unanimous vote of confidence and the opportunity you have given me. However, I think it politic for all concerned to let the present situation remain until I am officially exonerated. I wish to say too at this time, that I believe Mr. Finch was correct in his difficult decision, although I wouldn't have said that yesterday morning. I would also like to ask if there is to be an official internal enquiry."

The Chairman replies,

"I've spoken to the Director of Education in Northellington and he advises me that we must await the outcome of the Police investigations and then decide if that's necessary."

The Chairman looks around the table to include all members.

"I think I speak for us all here today, when I say I'm sorry you will not return to your duties for the moment, but appreciate the reasons influencing that decision. If there's no other business in connection with this matter, I'll bring the meeting to an end. Thank you for your time Ladies and Gentlemen. Good afternoon."

Several board members, many of them parents of pupils past and present, waylay Tom to offer their personal good wishes and support. Matthew Cross punches his arm and Richard Halton reminds him,

"Don't forget the meeting Thursday. I'll see you there."

CHAPTER EIGHT. BLACK THURSDAY.

Tom rings Will Metcalfe on Thursday morning, "Have you solved the case Will? Am I in the clear yet?"

"Afraid not Tom. There are one or two technicalities."

"What does that mean for heaven's sake?"

"Well for one thing, Papa Grayson won't give his consent to our seeing Annette by herself. We've interviewed them together at home and they both stick to their story."

"So, can't you split them up or can you see her with her mother instead?"

"He won't allow that either. We have to get a court injunction to see her without her parents you see and that will be through by this afternoon. Hang on Tom, we'll soon have you off the hook. Sorry it's taking longer than we thought."

Tom's mother rings as soon as he puts down the phone.

"Tom, instead of leaving the lawns until Saturday, why don't you come over and cut the grass today if you're still in limbo. If this is all over, you might be able to get away at the weekend. I suppose there's no news yet?"

Tom relays the latest from Will and then agrees to go over and do the chores.

Tom spends all Thursday morning at his mothers. He mows her grass front and back and trims the edges. There is usually a list of jobs for him, which he tries to fit in during weekends and it's good to be able to do them in the week. Perhaps all this will be over tomorrow and he will have the weekend free. They could all go off somewhere, camping maybe.

He borrows a ladder from the man next door and cleans out all the guttering round his Mother's bungalow.

"Mr. Forrest gave me another water barrel Tom. Would you be able to fit it by the side of the bathroom window do you think? We have to save as much rainwater as we can for the summer."

"Mm. I'll have to tap into that down pipe and fix an overflow. I'll nip down to the builder's merchants and see if they have a piece of pipe for that. Yes, it shouldn't be too hard."

Mother and son sit in the garden in the warm sunshine sipping their coffee. Inevitably the conversation turns to his suspension.

"I wish the police would declare their intentions one way or the other Tom, this waiting must be nerve wracking for you. They don't seem to be trying very hard."

"They must be letting things simmer for a while."

"Well, I don't know about simmering, things are just about boiling. You're missing an important time from school too."

"Yes but I'm just thankful the exams are over, at least the ones that matter are. Well, I'll be off to see Jack Timms."

" I haven't seen that man in ages, tell him I still live in the same house when he has time to call Tom and remember me to him."

When Tom draws into the old railway buildings, which now serve as a builder's merchants, Jack the proprietor, is on the forecourt chatting to a local joiner. His face lights up when he sees Tom park the car and he comes over to greet him.

"Hello there my lad. I've been hearing stories about you. What's going on up in the town then?"

"Hi there Uncle Jack, we have to liven things up a bit now and then. Good for tourism."

Tom's father and Jack were sucked into the war together, both in the R.A.F. Jack returned but Thomas was spewed out in the air cover over Dunkirk somewhere. Tom as his posthumous baby only knows his father as a legend. Jack is his father's buddy and also Tom's godfather.

"How's your mother taking this upset? I should think she's spitting cobs and wanting to set about somebody."

"Yes, you're right. She also reminds you that she is still resident in the same house."

"Sparky as ever eh!"

Tom tells the burly overalled figure about his predicament, as they walk into the warehouse and stays chatting for a while after making his purchases.

"Cheerio Uncle Jack. Ma sends her regards. Perhaps you'd better call soon and stop her sending out a posse."

"Leaning into the car window as Tom prepares to drive off, Jack asks,

"It's really serious then lad is it?"

"Yes Jack. It's serious and just now I'm unable to help myself, which is frustrating. I have to leave it to the law."

When Tom reaches home the school number is on the list of callers and with his heart playing leapfrog, he returns the call. The secretary in reception takes the call and puts him through to Peter Finch. The headmaster's voice comes over the line,

"Headmaster here."

"Tom Prescott. You rang me Sir. Sorry to miss your call."

"Hello there Tom, I wanted to thank you for your supportive comment yesterday. That meant a lot to me. Amidst your troubles, you could see my difficult position. Thank you. How are you feeling after the vote of confidence at the meeting?"

"That was heartening and appreciated."

"Are you keeping busy Tom?"

"There are a lot of overdue jobs to do for my mother and that's keeping me busy."

Something in the trivia of the conversation is ringing bells in Tom's head.

"Is anything wrong Sir?"

"No, nothing really wrong. I had Mr. Grayson on the rampage this morning. He found the girl missing and said he's sure you've kidnapped her. He's been round to your house Tom. I had to ring and ask the Police to warn him off. Annette has been absent from school since last week but they couldn't find her at home today and he thinks you've gone off together."

Thank God he'd been at his mothers'. If he'd opened the door to Grayson and been accused again, he might have hit him.

"Are you there Tom?"

"Yes Sir. Yes I'm here."

"I'm just warning you really to keep your head if you should meet him. Are there any developments yet? Have you heard anything from the Inspector?"

"No Sir. Sergeant Metcalfe told me they're waiting for a court order to interview the girl alone because Mr. Grayson won't give his permission."

"Apart from doing your mother's chores, how are you filling your free time Tom? Do you want me to send over some marking or programme structures to work on? I consider you are still on the staff even if you are not directly in contact. We miss you Tom and want you back with us as soon as possible."

"Thank you but I think I'll pass up the homework. I feel as though I have to be outdoors at the moment. Thank you for your support Sir, I appreciate it."

"Hmm," Tom muses silently as he put down the phone, "somebody has to fork out the cost of a supply teacher and it hurts."

CHAPTER NINE. THE WARM UP

Hazel spends Thursdays in Weybury. The mornings are taken up in the new County Primary school, adjacent to a new estate of private and association houses and flats. The old Primary school is Victorian and totally unsuitable for today's needs. Both the school and schoolhouse have been sold off, stripped inside and converted into executive apartments.

The new school accommodation is light, airy and modern, with an activity room where Hazel can teach in comfort. There are usually fifteen pupils taking music lessons here but not all of them are in the orchestra yet.

Weybury Comprehensive school takes the whole afternoon and she has to return on Friday mornings to complete the lessons. This school used to have a music teacher and its own orchestra, but with the financial cut-backs, that post was removed and the pupils came into her care. Now their orchestra is merged into the Dales Orchestra and the older pupils add a balance and stability to the younger children.

The first people to give their support are the receptionist and secretaries when she signs into school at nine a.m. Mrs Beales is next to commiserate with her on Tom's predicament.

"My dear Hazel, it's a crying shame for somebody like Tom to be in this situation. It's happening more and more these days I'm afraid, adolescent girls making up stories and causing trouble for teachers. If I can help in any way tell him to call me, he's known me long enough. I did speak to him on the phone yesterday; he sounded really cut up and no wonder. It isn't until they.re missing that you realize the large chunk of work somebody does and Tom's always done more than his share."

During the time spent in the school that afternoon several teachers and dinner ladies come in to speak to her and wish him well. Hazel asks them to give him a ring and cheer him up.

Hazel's last errand is to pick up the Darlington and Stockton Times and she parks in the bustling market square nearby. She notices Mrs Morton from the next village, walking towards her and sees her veer off to look in a shop window.

Hazel calls,

"Good afternoon," and receives a terse reply but nothing more. She stares at the woman in disbelief. This is a lady who always comes up to her to chat and exchange news on family members. But not today! Sadly, Hazel enters the cluttered shop.

"Hello Tricia. D & S. please."

The girl seems embarrassed and avoids Hazel's eyes as she passes the paper and takes the coins. She is usually chirpy and Hazel logs the fact she has no chat today. Perhaps people just don't know what to say so it's easier to say nothing. The same thing happens when folk meet a recently bereaved person. They cross over the road to avoid them because they can't handle the situation.

When she sits in the car and looks at the paper she sees the reason for Tricia's silence. The headlines shriek at her.

'Respected master suspended from Dales School'.

'Oh no. What will this do to him? He'll be mortified.' She hadn't even thought about it being splashed across the newspaper and is sure that Tom won't have. Why hadn't it occurred to her and *she* thinks Tom naïve. The salt tears smart in her eyes and she feels misery dribble through her as she imagines him reading the words swimming in front of her. There appear to be no names mentioned, but folk around here will know to whom the article refers. Should she leave the paper in the car until morning? Then others at the 'Wheatsheaf' would already have read it. He would see through that. No, he'd have to take it on the chin.

**

After lunch on Thursday Alex, David and Joe Prescott go down to the school farm office to help Harry Cross handle a new delivery of sheep nuts from The Farm Foods Company. The delivery has to be counted and checked against the invoice and the invoice entered into the school farm accounts book.

The school rent a 100-acre field from the next-door farmer who runs a dairy herd. Matthew Cross Harry's father, supervises the running of the school farm and it's small flock of Jacob's sheep, as a profit making enterprise. There is no gain from rearing Wensleydale sheep for meat, because of the hill farmers' crisis; low sheep prices and high cost of feed. That made Matt decide, that if Weybury pupils were to continue the advantage of this unique farming practice alongside academic subjects, they should change.

Jacob's fleeces are attracting much higher prices because of the upsurge in home industries and leisure activities like spinning and weaving. Slowly the farm is making profit, their breeding programme is on target and buyers for lambs and fleeces are approaching them rather than them going to the market place. Pupils making a career of farming and others with an interest, give their time on a rota at weekends and after school.

Their business completed, the four boys are returning to afternoon classes when they are waylaid by a group of year eleven lads, the same year as Annette Grayson. The harassment begins with cat calling towards Joe.

"Your Dad's a child molester."

"Your old man's kinky, all old men with odd eyes are wierdos."

"How does it feel when your Dad likes little girls? He's bent."

"He's a baby snatcher. Dirty old man." Joe protests.

"My Dad's innocent. He didn't touch her. Don't you talk about my Dad like that."

Joe feels sick and scared, his stomach churns with fear, but he isn't going to hear his Dad called names. The jeering turns to jostling and pushing him backwards and forwards between them. These lads are big fifteen-year-old youths with a longer reach than the thirteen year old friends. Rodney Needham the tallest lad, pushes Harry in the shoulder,

"We're not talking to you Cross, you and your pals scram. We just want to teach Prescott here a lesson in case he grows up like his old man. Has he been in her knickers yet Prescott?"

The other lads snigger and that's when Joe lashes out. He thumps a quick right and left at the lad's middle. The youth crumples and falls in a heap like a wet towel. Then fists and feet fly until an angry voice roars.

"Stop that NOW. Savages. All of you report to Mr. Finch's office and you'd better be there before I am, in three minutes. I've never seen such behaviour at this school before. Now scat."

Matthew Cross usually calls in the farm after his milk round to check on things and loses no time in joining the sorry looking group of pupils outside the Headmaster's door. One of them is his son.

**

Wendy arrives at Darlington College at ten- o-clock on Thursday morning. She knows she could have sent for a prospectus, but wants to see the set-up for herself. She always uses her

Dad's method of balancing the pros and cons of any situation, before making a decision. That entails making a list of points for and against each candidate and going for the winner. She knows too that both her parents will be disappointed if she doesn't go to Uni, especially Dad. Do they want it for her or for themselves? She'd thought this through on the bus coming up here and feels ashamed of the thought.

Although they left the decision to her, she is in no doubt as to their aspirations and she knows in her heart that they just want the best for her. Dad said, 'Take a year out if you want to get away from school, but get that Lit. Degree under your belt, then the world is your playground. It's what you are good at and it's what you always wanted to do.' He'd ruffled her hair and gone on, 'Teenage years are renowned for the bite of the love bug, but it doesn't just bite once, there will be other chances. It's part of growing up and learning about people. Get a job in a supermarket and see if that's what you want for the rest of your life.'

A small voice whispers in her head that she knows he's right and she still wants what she's always wanted. To write. Since as far back as she can remember, when Dad and Mum used to read to her, she could be as lost between the covers of a book as a grain of sand on the beach. From learning to read solo, she devoured everything that came her way, classics, rubbish, fact or fiction. Then Dad showed her how to digest as well as gobble, and to analyse and criticize what she read.

Brad is totally different and they really don't have much common ground. The initial attraction was purely physical. She supposes separating the flesh from what lies beneath, comes with maturity and practice. Brad does read and knows whether he likes a book, but can't say why. He doesn't read widely, but sticks to the authors he knows and the safe topics like crime and cowboys. A bit childish really, now she comes to think about it. His mind is numeric, travelling the track of percentages and stocks and shares. She soaks up history like kitchen roll. Geography and the world of travel holds her spellbound but leaves Brad unmoved. World markets and the FT index grab him by the throat while Wendy thinks it a list of Flowering Trees.

So why is she even considering this step? She'd never been into the boy scene until Brad sought her out and dated her. He aroused primeval emotions and pagan desires she hadn't know were there. Mum told her that is like wearing a new dress or tasting new food, the novelty wears off after a time. She knows there needs to be some enjoyable, shared ground to build on underneath the fleshy bits. His pushing, groping and fumbling cease to satisfy him lately and he's begun to pressure her to give him more.

"My parents always go to the British Legion club on Friday evenings. We could have the house to ourselves and could be alone together in comfort."

Brad said persuasively last time they met.

"If you love me, you'll give up this Uni rubbish and take a course here and then you can get a job until we get married and the babies come."

Wendy is aware this is emotional blackmail and knows she's not mature enough as yet, to shoulder the added burden of sexual experience. Some of her friends welcome it eagerly and change partners as often as hairstyles, but she feels that isn't right for her.

Picking up a prospectus from reception, Wendy obtains permission to look around the facilities. Grinning to herself, she thinks scanning the refectory is the first priority and of major importance.

"Something amusing you?" the deep voice at her side queries.

"Oh hello. I'm just doing a walk about and thought this a good place to start."
The well-shaped line in the face a foot above her, stretches into a wide grin,

"Well that's a practical beginning. The hard tack isn't bad and they don't rip you off. If you want a guide, I'm your man for ten minutes."

"Are you a student here?"

"Yes, in my last term. I've just done two years."

They take their plastic cups of coffee to an empty bench and sit on opposite sides of a formica topped table.

"The name's Simon. What are you going to do here?"

"I'm Wendy and I may not come at all. It's an option I'm considering. I've always thought I'd go to Uni and applied to Cambridge and St. Andrews. That's what my parents want for me too. My boyfriend wants me to take a course here instead, so I don't have to be away."

"What's your subject?"

"Literature or I could sidetrack to journalism."

"Mm. Well, if it were me, nobody would manipulate me that way. If you have the chance of a university place, take my advice and go for it. There's nothing like it here. It's a good move to leave home too and get out there."

"Oh? Perhaps you're right. At least I shall have had a look at what's on offer here."

"Come on I'll show you round."

Her companion lopes off at top speed with Wendy almost running to match his long strides. He shows her the I.T. suite where he is taking his graphics course and the floor above for commercial art and design. Journalism and advertising are part of this unit too, with social sciences on the floor above that.

"On the other side, there's the catering, body care and fashion departments. There's other stuff of course but they're satellite for Durham Uni. So there you have it Wendy. What will be the deciding factor do you think? The coffee shop?"

"Ha. I just don't know. Something will decide for me in the next week or two. Thank you for spending your coffee break on a guided tour, I do appreciate it Simon. Does term end this week?"

"Yup, tomorrow is my last day here. I've enjoyed it but it'll be good to be earning and hear a jingle in my pocket. Starting Friday, I shall be plodding around job hunting. I've written off for a few and have interviews for two. My portfolio is waiting for the highest bidder."

His eyebrows twitch and he grins at her.

"All the best Wendy and choose carefully."

"Thanks, I will. Good luck Simon with the job hunt. Cheers."

"I give him nine out of ten," Wendy thinks to herself, "I could grow to like him more than a bit. Very different to Brad."
That thought pulls her up short.

"Hey, what am I thinking about, I'm Brad's girl aren't I?"

One of the frequent buses deposits her in the town centre, where she makes several purchases. She picks up the Darlington and Stockton Times and then remembers Mum usually takes one home. Putting it back on the rack, the headline scorches along her optic nerve.

'Respected Master suspended from Dales School.'

It couldn't be. But it was. Snatching the paper from the stand again she scans the article. There are no names or places mentioned but the allegations against a master are front-page news. Wendy drops the paper as though the print is burning her fingers, but it seems every customer is buying a copy. Poor Dad. What must he be feeling? How can she even consider disappointing him by dealing him a further body blow?

Brad and she are seeing a film that evening, so she's surprised to see him waiting to meet her from the bus in Weybury market place.

"This is nice of you Brad."

"Yes, well you said you were going to Darlington and I guessed you'd make a day of it."

His voice sounds flat and tense.

"Is anything wrong? Has something happened?"

"Well, I've been thinking over what you told me about your Dad. Then if you're away at that university, I'll never see you. I might as well not have a girl friend. I think it better if we finish now."

Wendy stands still, staring at him in disbelief. The sullen expression on his handsome face and the defiant note in his voice scratches a raw nerve.

"I don't suppose that article in the D and S could have helped you make this decision?"

He looks like her brother when she catches him in her room and mumbles,

"It doesn't look good, does it? I didn't think about it getting into the papers."

"And you'd rather not be associated with us, is that it? It wouldn't look good at the bank would it? Well, that's OK by me and for your information, I didn't think about it being in the paper either. What a loyal friend you turned out to be. It's a good job I didn't rely on you for support. I can find my own way home thank you."

Mum, Dad and Joe are in the kitchen when Wendy reaches home and the three faces looking at her expectantly is more than she can take at that moment. Dropping her parcels on the floor, she pulls open the inner door and flies upstairs. Flopping on to her bed she lets the flood of tears swill away the hurt and anger, which have been festering like a boil over the past two days.

The storm passes and in the calm that follows, there is a tap at the door.

"It's Dad love. Can I come in?"

Swallowing a gulp, she answers quietly,

"Yes Dad."

Sitting beside her on the bed, her Dad put his arm around her.

"Can you tell me about it?"

Recounting how she saw the newspaper in W. & H. Smiths, then the conversation with Brad starts the tears afresh.

"Poor Dad. Having all those lies splattered over the front page. Even if they haven't named you, everyone around here knows who it's about. I'm sure Susie Smith didn't put it in, she'd have rung you first."

"Yes, she rang me this morning as soon as she knew, to warn me it would be headlines. She says that Grayson informed the editor direct and she tried to stop it but was too late. The paper will just have to make me headlines again when it's all cleared up, but next time I want my picture on the front page too."

Tom smiles at her and squeezes her fingers reassuringly,

"There's one good thing, it's now public. Before, we weren't sure who knew and who didn't. Tell me about your visit to the college. How did it go?"

Wendy reaches for a tissue to dab her eyes,

"Oh, alright. A nice guy showed me round, he's been doing graphics. They have a super I.T. suite but generally, I expected something better. You can stop worrying Dad, I'm going to Uni. I think I'd made up my mind before Brad gave me the brush-off."

"Poor darling. He's shown me what I always knew. That you're worth somebody better than Brad. He would have trapped you in marriage and Weybury before you had a chance to see anything else. If you come back here to live, I want it to be because you've chosen to." He hugs her closer.

"Does it hurt very much love?"

"Well, it was a shock Dad, the last thing I expected. Then I was mad and a bit relieved as well. He was beginning to be possessive and a bit, er demanding. Maybe it's just my pride that's hurt or perhaps I've simply grown out of him. I suppose he just proved that I'm able to attract a chap."

"Poppet, you can catch any fellow you want, you don't have to prove it. There's time for all that later. This is just a bit more growing up for you."

**

It's always a rush on Thursdays. Tea is in relays because Wendy is sometimes out, Joe has Scouts and his Dad has sports practice after school. Then he will be going to his cricket meeting in the 'Sheaf'.

The Scouts have their weekly bash in the Church Hall and because it is in the same direction as 'The Sheaf' Tom and Joe walk together. When Tom hurries off Joe's best mate Alex Brown meets him with,

"Hi Joe. Everybody's asking me about your Dad. My Dad always says, you shouldn't believe all you read in the papers. Anyway, I don't believe he did that and neither do my folks."

"Thanks Alex. Mind you, the paper doesn't say who's accused or use names. It just says a master has been suspended pending enquiries."

"We got off lightly this afternoon didn't we? I wouldn't want to be in Rodney Needham's shoes would you? They'll get detention for a week at least I should think. Hey, your face is pretty Joe, does it hurt?"

Some of the other lads are looking at him, whispering behind their hands and sniggering. He doesn't know whether they've heard about the fight and are looking at his swollen eye or if it's his Dad's bother. Then the meeting begins and Arkela calls them to order.

David Dean won't speak to him all evening but as they are leaving the hall, his mother stops Joe. He can smell her scent and hear the huge bracelets she wears, jangling as she moves her arm.

"Hello Joe, you've been fighting I hear. I'm glad I've caught you. I have to tell you there won't be room for you when we go camping after all. I'm so sorry and it's a shame to disappoint you, but David's cousin decided at the last minute that he wanted to come and then there's all the luggage you see."

"Yes Mrs Dean, I see. Doesn't matter anyway. Dad's going to take me."

Joe can't believe his ears. She couldn't be saying this. It's only the other day David and he were discussing what they needed to take for the trip. His eyes prickle, he feels sick and wants to run home. He bends down and reties his shoelace. David's father Phillip Dean, is a fellow teacher with Joe's Dad and they are going camping to Robin Hood's Bay in the summer holidays. Because their Melissa is going on holiday with a cousin, Mrs Dean told David he could take a friend along and Joe was his choice.

Joe had been surprised the Dean's were going camping. They were both a bit, well, posh and Mrs Dean put all that paint on her face and fingernails. When Joe dabbled with their Wendy's stuff, it took a lot of scrubbing off and made his face sore. Maybe she didn't put it on every day, perhaps it lasted a few days. Anyway, he couldn't imagine her cooking bacon over a camp stove with all those rings and stuff getting in the way.

They weren't as easy going as Joe's parents. He'd been to their house to play with David a few times but it didn't feel right and he knew David would rather come to his place. Next to Alex, David is his best mate. Anyway, his own Dad always takes him cycling and hiking and might take him camping if he asks him. He wouldn't have time to go with the Deans anyway.

He feels Alex grab his arm,

"Come on, I'll race you home."

Alex lives in the same direction as Joe and the two boys tear off together.

"What will you be doing when we break up Alex?"

"I think the first week we'll be going down to Grans in Norfolk, we usually do. It's O.K. there but a bit boring. There's nobody to play with. I don't know what else we'll do. Is your Dad really taking you camping?"

Joe looks embarrassed and shrugs his shoulders,

"Oh, I just said that, but I'll ask him if he will. If he says yes, will you come with us?"

Alex stops in his tracks and grabs Joe's sleeve.

"Will I? That'd be terrific. Hey. You know, your eye's really stunning now. It's going all purple right across to your nose and down your face and there's some pink gooey juice in the corner."

**

Will Metcalfe is already in the back room of the 'Wheatsheaf' or the 'Snug' as it's known, when Tom walks in. It's always a surprise to see

Will wearing neither his uniform nor cricket whites but his energy is no less because he's dressed casually. Tom pans the gathering of men at the bar, says a general

"Good evening," before joining Will and Jim Iveson the landlord, in rearranging the tables for the meeting. Jim returns to his bar and Will says,

"I'm glad I've seen you on your own Tom, I'll tell you this in confidence because I'm not supposed to discuss the case. Do you know Annette Grayson's done a bunk?"

"Ye-es, I do know. Peter Finch rang at lunch time to tell me. He said you had to apprehend Grayson. Is that right Will?"

"That's correct. He saw Annette's bag was missing and rang the school to check if she was there. He was told that Annette was marked

173

absent. He didn't believe she wasn't there and went up to see Finch. He accused Finch of lying to him and that Annette was hiding in school. He threatened to tear the place apart until he found her. When Finch finally convinced him that Annette hadn't been seen since last week, he immediately thought you'd gone off with her."

Both men are setting out the chairs around the tables placing the large carver at the head of the table for the Chairman.

He continues,

"Apparently the man was beside himself, ranting and raving about what he was going to do to everybody and rushed out of the school shouting he was going round to your place to have it out. Finch rightly rang us and I went to your house and sure enough he was banging on your doors and raising the roof. He'd really flipped. Now he's cooling off in our lock up awaiting the magistrates pleasure for causing a disturbance."

Tom sits on a stool to let the news sink in.

"Whew! I didn't know it was that bad. Some news escapes the bush telegraph then. I was jobbing at Mum's and missed all this thank heavens. I'm not surprised Annette left though. What puzzles me is why she didn't go before."

"Mm. Perhaps opportunity didn't present itself. Anyway, she was absent Tuesday and I saw her at home with her father in the evening. There was a bruise on her face then, said she'd fallen in the gym at school. I wonder now whether he'd been a bit rough with her. She was off school yesterday too, but went as usual this morning. Grayson must have nipped back into the house to check and that's when he realized she'd gone."

Will heaves two more chairs up to a table before continuing,

"Now one of the girls in the paper shop tells me she saw Annette getting on the Richmond bus this morning. We have a court injunction, which enables us to set up an interview without her parents tomorrow morning but that looks as though it's off. We were hoping to get this cleared up and you in the clear before the weekend."

This conversation comes to an end when cricket club members begin arriving and the committee take their places round the table. Philip Dean takes his seat at the head flanked by the secretary and treasurer with committee members either side. The team members arrayed around the table make it unique and public, rather than just a committee meeting. It is this that Philip Dean wants to change to a more orthodox and private arrangement. Matt is chatting to Tom when Philip leaves his chair and comes over to them. His serious face wears a benevolent expression as he addresses Tom.

"Tom, I've cancelled the squash match tomorrow and I've scratched your name from the team for the present. I didn't think you'd want to be playing with all this going on. I wonder whether it might be a good idea for you to resign as captain of the cricket team too."

Tom's face registers his shock and humiliation. He flinches and feels his face stretch and his eyes widen, but after a second replies calmly,

"Thanks for the vote of confidence Philip but actually, I like to be consulted in advance about important issues like this, not to be sprung on like a Jack in the box with my fate already decided for me and in public too."

Matt dives in to the altercation,

"I'll tell you this for free *Mr*. Chairman. If you insist on Tom resigning, you won't have a cricket team, but by all means put it to the meeting."

"Well there's no need to be like that about it. I'm only doing my job as I see it and trying to save Tom embarrassment."

"Then do it in the correct manner and let's get this meeting started."

Matt grabs Tom by the arm and marches him over to sit beside him, half way down the table muttering,

"Bloody hypocrite."

A flushed and fidgety Philip Dean takes the Chairman's seat again and calls the meeting to order.

"An emergency matter has arisen. As I am sure you are all aware, our Captain is helping the Police with some inquiries and at the moment is suspended from his school duties. I have suggested that he may like to stand down as Captain for the moment until it's been sorted out, but the final decision lies with you, the committee and team members. Will all those in favour of Tom Prescott remaining as team Captain, please raise their hands?"

Around ten men are sitting around the table and after a moment of shocked silence, not only every hand except one is raised, but every man but one stands up. Ralph Brumpton's face is the picture of embarrassed discomfort, made worse by the deadly looks and silent censure of his colleagues. The men standing around the table stamp their feet and the noise in the room is deafening.

"Er, yes. I see we have almost one hundred per cent in favour of Tom continuing to lead the team. Thank you gentlemen, now we will proceed to the first item on the agenda, which is of course selecting that team."

The men ignore him and talk among themselves, expressing in their direct way, the indignation they are feeling. Matthew Cross raises his hand.

"I request permission to speak Mr. Chairman."

Receiving a nod from Philip he continues,

"Perhaps I'm prejudiced in Tom's favour because I've known him since we were lads. I know he's innocent as I suspect do most of you. On his behalf, I thank those of you who raised your hands, for your support. Tom's a good Captain, we have a good and loyal team and I for one, see no reason to change that. Thank you."

Cheers bounce from the walls of the 'snug' and a mortified Philip Dean bangs on his gavel to bring the meeting to order.

Tom is overwhelmed. A rush of warm affection and gratitude for these men, most of whom he's known for all of his life, warms him. He feels his eyes prick and something sticks in his throat. The unjustness of his enforced situation suddenly recedes into the distance as love for his fellow townspeople swamp his being. Incapable of words, he simply raises his hands in acknowledgement.

**

After Tom and Joe leave on Thursday evening, Hazel sits down at the table in the sitting room window, to do some transcribing for the next day. Friday mornings are spent at the Comprehensive school until break before going on to see four pupils at the Roman Catholic primary school, also in Weybury. Because she needs a lot of time to go over to Millburn, she leaves the afternoon for that. Music transcribing takes time and if she does that tonight she can sleep easier. She can persuade the secretary to photocopy the manuscripts tomorrow in school. She really needs to be full time to fit in all the schools with the written work too and the extra hours are available if she wants them. Life is much easier for everybody at home if she stays with four days and she is trying very hard to do this.

Isabel calls in on her way home from visiting a friend and stays for a coffee. Wendy and Amy are struggling with a dress pattern laid out on the floor.

"Gran, you're good at sewing aren't you? I bought the amount of material it says but forgot it has a pattern. What can I do?"

"Well, I don't think I can get down there, or rather I won't get up again if I do." Isabel leans over the pattern and points to the folded material.

"Try laying your material with just enough to fit in the back piece to the fold and cut that out. Then you'll have a larger piece for the fronts and the sleeves and bits will come out of the rest. Lay it out and see."

A deafening crash splinters the busy scene and a large stone bounces off the table and onto the pattern. Glass splatters over the table and chairs and a gaping hole shows where the window once was. Fortunately for Hazel the broken window is at the opposite end to where she is sitting.

Amy is the first to recover. She leaps to her feet and runs to the front door. Yanking it open, she sprints out into the road. There is nobody to be seen except old Mr. Burrows from a few doors up.

"Did you see anybody throwing stones Mr Burrows? Someone's just lobbed one through Tom's window."

"Four or five lads just jumped over yon school wall but I didn't see no stone throwing. Put one through Tom's winder you say? It's a bit of a devil. Don't know what this town's coming to. Do you want a hand wi' owt? I've some sheets of plastic like, what'd fit yon window."

Wendy joins them on the footpath,

"Thank you Mr. Burrows. That's very kind of you and such a help. Dad's out at his cricket meeting. I think he has some masking tape in the garage, we could fix your plastic sheet on with that couldn't we?"

"Aye, owt like that'll hold it until your Dad can have it fixed. I reckon one of them lads were that great gawk of Needhams but I couldn't swear to it."

While Hazel and Isabel clear up the glass inside the house, Mr. Burrows and the girls bring steps and stick the plastic onto the window frame.

"That's wonderful Mr. Burrows. Dad will be ever so grateful."

"Well it looks nowt, but it'll keep weather out until tomorrer like. Looks like there's a storm blowing up an all."
The old chap looks at Wendy,

"There's nowt like hitting a bloke when e's down. Your poor Dad 'as enough on his platter wi'out 'ooligan trouble. You tell 'im if I can help 'e just 'as to ask."

"Thanks again Mr. Burrows, I'll tell Dad."

Gran has shaken the fated material free of glass splinters and Hazel is whizzing round the carpet with the vacuum cleaner.

"I'm putting the kettle on again Mum, I think we need a fix."

Isabel cuts her finger on a stray shard of glass and explodes,

"That's it. I'll be down to see that Inspector in the morning. It's high time they had this business cleared up. If they got on with break-ins and this kind of thing as keenly as they get on to the motorist, it would have been stopped before reaching this stage. It seems decent people can't live in peace anymore."

The flags are flying in Isabel's cheeks and she wraps a tissue around her finger to mop the bleeding until Hazel puts on a sticking plaster.

The two women and their young companions drink their coffee huddled round the fire, talking in whispers. They couldn't have explained why they are speaking in hushed voices, it just fits the scene. After the initial shock and clearing up, the girls abandon their pattern and when Hazel asks,

"Why are we whispering?" they collapse in a heap of giggles.

"Be-because we're not double glazed any more and big brother might be listening outside our new fix-it-quick window." Wendy splutters helplessly against Amy's shoulder.

"Joe will be home any minute. I'm not allowed to meet him now he's so grown up. He and his pal Alex Brown walk most of the way together and we don't think they can come to much harm in the light evenings."

Hazel collects the coffee mugs and turns to Isabel,

"You haven't seen Joe's shiner have you Gran? He got set on at school and stuck up for Tom."

"That's outrageous. I hope that Finch fellow caught the thugs. To set on to a child like that!"

Hazel grins at Isabel's defence of her family.

"Yes he knows the culprits. Actually Matt Cross saw what happened and sent them all to the Headmaster's office."

Isabel grumbles,

"I expect that Finch would pat them on the head and tell them to go away and be good boys. No discipline these days."

Joe is just coming in the door as Hazel reaches the kitchen and she listens quietly when he tells her of his disappointment and she puts her arms round him and hugs him.

"Don't be too upset love, sometimes when you're let down, something better comes along. We'll ask Dad in the morning. He may be a bit late tonight. You know what these cricket meetings are like."

Isabel is flicking through a magazine when Hazel enters with Joe. She notices he is looking down in the mouth then sees his eyes widen as he spots the makeshift window arrangement.

"Why's that plastic up at the window Mum?"

His sister tells the story and that on top of his recent disappointment upsets Joe even more. He goes over to sit very close by his Gran.

"Why would somebody do that? Throw a rock I mean. Who do you think it was? Do you think they'll come back again when it's dark?" Isabel puts her arm around the boy, so much like Tom. She hugs him close,

"No dear, I don't think for one moment they'll be back again. We don't know who it was but Mr. Burrows saw some big lads go over the school wall."

Joe twiddles his scout badge.

"Is it to do with Dad's fuss?"

"I should think so love. You don't have to worry, nobody's after you."

She squeezes his arm gently,

"Your Dad's going to be mad when he sees the mess they made of the window."

The unfairness of this whole matter provokes her anger again. That a little lad should be set upon by a gang of hoodlums and beaten for something that silly chit dreamed up, is disgraceful.

"Did you have a good meeting Joe? What did the boys say when they saw your pretty face?"

"My pals all had a good look at it. Alex said he'd like one if it was just for a day and it didn't hurt."

"Well, he was there wasn't he? He should have got in the way instead of you." Isabell suddenly stands and looks at Amy,

"Goodness, look at the time. Are you going home Amy? I'll walk along with you if you'll have me."

It is just after one o'clock when Hazel hears the first clap of thunder. She doesn't know if that is what wakened her or if she'd sensed

Tom's side of the bed was empty. After a few minutes a sharp flash beams across the room, showing every object in a blue light. It is chased immediately by another deafening crash of thunder, which grumbles loudly away over the rooftops. She slips from the bed, into a wrap and pads down the stairs. Tom is in the kitchen staring through the window at the rain lashing the trees. It is thudding on the porch roof like bullets and bouncing on the patio with torrential fury. Each drop seems to burst on the windowpane as if jetted from a water pistol.

Can't sleep love?"

"Sorry, did I wake you? I did sleep for a while, and then I dreamed I was drowning. You know when you have a dream like that, it continues after you wake up and you lay there trying to finish the scene?" he spreads his hands and looks at her as if for confirmation.

"Anyway, I couldn't get back to sleep. I expect I must have heard the rain in the dream." Hazel puts her arm round his middle and they stand together watching the storm. The next flash bounces through the window with such a power surge, they can see to the bottom of the stairs. They both jump back from the window.

"Hey that's close."

The sharp, ear-smashing crack of thunder overhead is immediate, simultaneous with an explosion and the crash and rumble of falling masonry.

"Something's been hit and it's nearby. Pass my coat Hazel and I'll take a look outside."

Tom forces his bare feet into wellingtons, tucking in his pyjama legs. The gale force winds blast into the kitchen when he opens the outside door and he recoils under the force, to gather his wits. An acrid smell of sulphur drifts in as he disappears into the night, pulling the door closed. Hazel goes to look around the sitting room to see if the replacement window is holding up and catches Joe tumbling down the stairs, two at a time. His hair is sticking up in spikes and his eyes round with terror, he hurtles into her arms.

"Have they come back Mum. What's all that crashing? What's happened? Where's Dad?"

"Hold on there Joe boy it's just a thunder storm, but the crash you heard was bricks falling outside. The lightening must have struck something and Dad's gone to see. Isn't it exciting?"

Hazel pulls Tom's sweater over Joe's head, where it droops like a sack on a scarecrow and pulls him towards the kitchen.

"We don't usually have storms like this 'Downdale'. Come and watch with me through the window, it's brilliant."

The door flies open and Tom catapults inside pulling a bundle wrapped in an old coat.

"Ginny's chimney took that blast and burned out her television set. It struck the aerial. I've sent for the fire brigade but I think the fire's already out. Bricks everywhere and a hole in the roof."

Hazel takes the coat and reveals their elderly neighbour.

"Come to the fire Ginny, it is Ginny underneath there? You can finish the night in Joe's room or on the bed-settee, whichever you like. I've opened up the Aga and the kettle's on the boil."

Hazel collects tea pot and cups and pulls the steaming kettle off the heat.

"I expect your electricity will be off with the blast, ours is. Wasn't it a bang? Blew Joe out of his bed, didn't it love?"

Joe is feeling braver now he's with people and not alone in his bedroom. He clutches Tom's sweater round him like a life jacket. Grinning at Ginny he says,

"You can sleep in my room Ginny, it's a good bed and I can look after you there."

Ginny settles into a chair with Hazel's old woolly jacket round her shoulders, beaming at everybody,

"What it is to have wonderful neighbours like you. I'm so lucky. I wondered what on earth was happening: I thought an atom bomb had come and was never so pleased to see anybody in my life as I was to see Tom."
She picks up the mewling kitten and hugs it to her chin.

"I bet you're wondering what's going on little kitty but you're safe here with all of us."

The Aga is turned on to full heat and the cosy kitchen is warm as a nest. As usual, they sit around the big pine table in whatever they have found to throw on, as though waiting for a meal at a fancy dress party.

"Now, who wants what to drink? We have Horlicks, drinking chocolate, tea or camomile tea and hot milk. I don't think coffee's a very good idea at this time of night. What would you like Ginny?"

Wendy stumbles through the door to join the party, having slept through most of the noise,

"What am I missing? Looks like a midnight feast. Hello Ginny, what happened to you?"

"Ginny's been bombed out and you didn't hear a thing."

Tom rumples his daughter's hair,

"I bet it was only the kettle whistling that woke you."

The wail of the fire engine speeding up the road adds flavour to the party as it pulls up at the front of the houses, with a screech of brakes.

"I expect the lads will appreciate a hot drink after being on your roof Ginny. I'll just nip out and see them, might persuade them to patch that hole up with a sheet of plastic."

Tom knows all the firemen, several of whom are cricket chums and some of the others old school mates. The storm is passing along to the upper Dale now; he can see the flashes and the thunder further to the west. The wind is less fierce and the rain gentler, but the night isn't the best to be clambering over a roof on slippery slates. There are four firemen, each dressed in full regalia and they hail the comic sight of Tom floundering around in his ancient gardening gear.

"Hi there lover boy. You on night shift then or looking for pretty maidens to ravish? Bloody shame. Couldn't have picked a less likely bloke. You mauling a schoolgirl? Never heard such tripe. Now then what's to do here?" When the crew have made everything safe they troop in to the kitchen and are fed and watered and pulling Ginny's leg about bombs and disasters forcing her exile. As the men leave Jack Woods prods Tom in the shoulder,

" Keep your end up lad, it'll soon be over and then we can get you back to work. Thanks for refreshments Hazel. Keep smiling. No more bombs tonight Ginnie. Sleep well. Night."

Much later, when everybody is settled into bed and the storm has died away, Tom and Hazel lay softly talking in the dark.

"Poor Ginny she'll have a mess to clear up in the morning, especially if the firemen thought fit to make sure there's no risk of fire by dousing what's left of the chimney. At least I'll be able to help her. We can't blame anybody for a natural disaster, but it's strange how things come all at once." Tom nuzzles his nose in her neck.

"You know love, it wouldn't be so bad if it were just me they were getting at, but I just hate the way this nightmare's affecting the kids. Young Joe's being persecuted and we know how cruel kids can be. Poor lad's as jumpy as a flea. Our property's under attack and Wendy's love life's in tatters. I can only imagine what it's like for you trying to keep us all from looping the loop."

Hazel strokes his hair,

"I wouldn't worry too much about Wendy love. She'll bounce back as always. In fact Brad did us all a big favour. Joe will recover and this will all fade with time. My shoulders can bear the burden, I've been in tight corners before. Poor Tom. It must be like watching a horror movie with yourself as centre stage."

"Something like that. I simply cannot believe that some people think I did this. You go along living your life in your ideal world, doing the job you love, not thinking about how you appear to other people, how they see you and what they think of you. Then wham. One below the belt and the town's taking sides. Some see you as a monster who should be run out of town and others stand by you."

Hazel cuddles up closer and trails gentle fingers down his face.

"The cricket meeting left you with good feelings though, didn't it?"

"Yes, it did after the initial shock. I'll be forever grateful for Matt. That guy goes straight for the jugular and says what he thinks. There couldn't be a more loyal friend. I was so overcome, I couldn't stand up and thank them. Imagine that! Me, speechless! I couldn't believe the support was unanimous, except for Brumpton of course. He looked as if he wished he were anywhere but there. He might as well shut up shop for a week or two, because he'll lose custom there's no doubt of that."

"What were your reasons for not taking up the offer of reinstatement at yesterday's meeting? That was a vote of confidence too wasn't it?"

There's a pause as Tom considers this,

"Well, there were one or two reasons really. There were a couple of members yesterday who were a bit unsure. One is a parent and the other a councilor. If I returned without a clean bill of health, I would still be under a cloud. The world has to know I'm innocent for my own sake as well."

Hazel whispers sleepily,

"The people who really know you, know you couldn't possibly be guilty and they've stood up to be counted love. This nightmare will soon be over. You'll see. Just stick with it a bit longer."

"I've been wondering how many poor devils have been in my position and judged guilty. Their careers ruined and their lives wrecked because of some accusation, some girlish fantasy. It would mean moving house and neighbourhood, uprooting families, losing a good pension and beginning all over again."

"Now look here Tom Prescott, nothing like that is going to happen to you. Just don't think of it."

They talk a few minutes longer then arms wrapped around each other, snuggle down to sleep.

CHAPTER TEN. RECKONING

"Are you not eating breakfast Joe? What's the matter son?"

"Not hungry Dad."

"Am I hearing correctly? Is this Joe Prescott speaking?"

Joe tries to grin but doesn't manage it very well. He looks peaky and tired and his bruised eye shines like a flag.

Hazel and Wendy are looking tired but otherwise normal with appetites intact.

Tom looks as though he'd just got out of bed but he keeps the ball rolling.

"That's a splendid shiner you have there my lad, I bet there were some envious looks at Scouts last night."

He traces his finger gently around the discolouration on Joe's face, now glowing in brilliant technicolour over one eye and half of his face.

"Mum tells me Mrs Dean can't take you camping now Joe. I know you're disappointed about that, but do you know? I'm pleased. A friend of mine has a boat on the river at Skipton and he says we can borrow it for a week. If Will Metcalfe can give me some idea whether there's going to be a blasted court case or not, we can fix a date. You could ask Alex if he wants to come. Be company for you."

"Wow Dad. A boat. That'd be great. I know Alex would love to come if they're not at his Grans."

"We'll sort something out about that, don't worry".

Joe's face brightens at this and he valiantly attacks his toast again.

"Let's take a look at the score."

Tom counts the items on his fingers,

"Looks as if Wednesday and Thursday were bad days. Last night Phillip Dean asked me to stand down as team captain until this matter's cleared up. There was uproar and he was over-ruled. He's dropped me from the squash team and cancelled the game we had today. Says something urgent came up. He's a devious chap is our Phillip.

His finger count is now two.

"The do with the butchers and the Misses Stott are all on the down side. The window could be put down to youthful spite, must ring Tony Brown about replacing it this morning."

He makes a memo on a piece of scrap paper.

"Now where were we? Yes. Poor Joe had a tough day, his scars are there to show his bravery. Wendy had a turn yesterday. Do you want to add your bit love?"

"There's only Joe doesn't know that Brad's ditched me. Apart from a few funny looks as if I'm to be pitied. Then the shock of seeing the article in the D.& S. that's all I can add. Oh James rang last night and he'd seen the D & S, so up there in Durham the natives know all about things. How does our wounded warrior feel this morning?"

"My eye hurts and I feel a bit sick."

Joe pushes his remaining toast to the edge of his plate and slumps in his chair

"Have a bit more toast Joe, it helps to take off the sickness. Of course, speaking as a mother, I can't be sorry that Brad's out of the picture. I never thought he was good enough for you anyway. I'm sorry you're feeling very hurt and let down and I do think it may not have happened if it wasn't for Dad's situation."
Hazel puts the fruit bowl on the table then sits to eat her own breakfast.

"At least we're finding out who are our genuine friends. Nothing much has happened to me directly. There have been a few pitying looks and groups of people gossiping that broke up when I came along. Apart from that, there has been support from all the schools Tom and a vote of confidence from Polly Baxter and staff at Tamthorne. You're not suspended from her school. She'll have told you that herself I'm sure. More people are for you than against you and I'm sure some people don't know what to say."

Hazel spreads marmalade thickly on her buttered toast and takes an appreciative bite.

"They may seem against you simply because they're embarrassed. It does worry me this feeling of opposing sides and I think it will be a long time before the damage is forgotten."

Hazel looks round her beloved family. Poor Joe with a bruised eye and cheek, no wonder he feels sick. Her lovely daughter appears undamaged by her broken romance, the violet eyes sparkle, the auburn hair is neatly brushed and a smile curves her lips. James Halton's phone call last night continued for a long time. James is Rick Halton's son and since they were small children had been protective of Wendy. He is studying marine biology at Durham University and home for holidays soon. He will be good for her daughter just now. Then she looks at Tom's ravaged face. This business is crucifying him. He'd been up again in the night after their adventure.

Watching him this morning, she finds it hard to believe a person can look so different in a few days without some dreadful illness. He'd risen early for a run, showered and eaten breakfast, but instead of looking refreshed and ready for anything as he normally does, he looks haggard and worn out. As Hazel pours more tea, she hears the post plop through the box and sees Wendy make her usual dive for the letters.

"Hm. None for me again." Joe grumbles struggling through a bite of toast.

"Perhaps if you wrote some, you might have replies." His sister quips ruffling his coppery head and handing the one letter to Tom. He slits the envelope and withdraws a single sheet of paper. Hazel hears his quick indrawn breath and watches the colour drain from his face. She puts her hand on his arm and he passes her the letter. There's no address and it is typewritten, unsigned and to the point.

"Dad, Mum? What is it?"
Wendy feels the shock and horror slithering across the table like thick slime. Hazel passes her the letter and she reads out loud,

"We don't want paedophiles in this town. Get out."

"What's a peedo whatsit Mum?"

214

"A person who does bad things to children."

"Like what sort of bad things. Like going inside their knickers?"

There is a short pause while Hazel digests this.

"Yes things like that, to boys as well as girls. How did you know?"

"That's what Rodney Needham asked if Dad did."

Tom raises his head,

"Is that what the fight was about son?"

"Yes Dad. I got mad and thumped him."

"Thank you Joe. I call that real courage."

"I can't go to school this morning Dad. I feel sick."

**

Breakfast at the Dean's is a quiet formal occasion and doesn't commence until Melissa, David and their parents are seated promptly at eight a.m. There is rarely any conversation and never any laughter or fun. This morning however, Mavis Dean speaks to the newspaper on the opposite side of the table,

"Have the Police charged Tom Prescott yet Philip?"

"No, nothing's happened so far."
The paper doesn't waver and the disembodied voice comes from behind it to answer her questions.

"Do you think he did it?"

"I really don't know. They say there's no smoke without fire, so perhaps he did."

"He's a colleague of yours, you should know him as well as anybody."

"What does that signify? Paedophiles don't advertise their activities. He's certainly popular with the girls in school. You'd expect a Senior Master to be stricter and act more appropriately to his position."

Melissa ventures,

"Daddy, Annette Grayson made it all up. Mr. Prescott didn't touch her."

"Yes he did, he touched both you and Annette. What do you know about it anyway? Get on with your breakfast,"

"Yes Daddy, he touched us both at Whitby, but he didn't do the other."

"How do you know that?"

Melissa hurries on before Philip can say more.

"I just know. I think her father beats her, she's terrified of him."

"What nonsense. I want to hear no more of this."

Philip throws down The Times and scraping his chair on the floor, pushes away from the table and stalks out of the kitchen.

"Sorry Mum, but it's true. I'm sure she made it up. Mr Prescott's a good teacher and we all wish he was back."

**

Mrs Cross is in Denis Pratt's bakery shop, when she hears the latest. She always shops early on Fridays to avoid the crush of market day. She has to fit it in between the bottle sterilizing and Matt coming home for his second breakfast, after the milk round. He's always starving and likes a bacon butty with fresh crusty buns. Isabel Prescott is buying her granary loaf and Denis Pratt is wrapping it up.

"There you go Isabel. Is Tom off the hook yet?"

"No he's not and I shall have words with that Inspector Shaw on my way home. They don't seem to be doing anything to help him. Do you know, yesterday was terrible. Last night while I was there, he had a lump of stone through the front window."

"Is that a fact? That's shocking. There are some strange people in this town these days. When I was a lad, the local bobby knew the ones who caused trouble and he knew their fathers. Nowadays, if they catch 'em, they let 'em off or they get community service. I could give 'em some community service round here."

"I'm so sorry to hear of Tom's trouble Mrs Prescott."

Sandy Cross helps Isabel to stow her purchases into her basket.

"I'd never have believed people in Weyburne could be so vicious and to such a nice family. It must be dreadful for them all."

"Folk are violent these days, look at them lager louts."

Knowing Matt's partiality for his crusty buns, Denis Pratt is already putting a dozen in paper bags.

"Too much television in my opinion."

"That's right Denis. Yes Sandy, it's been a terrible week for them and I feel so helpless. I want to shake somebody. I shall go and see that Inspector straight away."

Josh Eastwood is in his shop by five a.m. to unlock the rear door for the two lads. He is always earlier on Friday mornings because it is market day and very busy. The girls come in at eight thirty when the shop opens. Most of his meat is reared and killed locally and all the food in his shop is of the very highest quality. He has to be ready for those who shop on their way to work. Large quantities of sausage meat, minced beef and a staggering amount of choice meats, cooked and uncooked are laid out behind the glass display counters. The smell of pasties, custard and fruit pies, quiches and other pastries fill the air, mingling with the red meat and cleaning fluid smell.

In the Eastwood household, breakfast is a quiet time, with just Kath and their young Mandy. Kath Eastwood notices Mandy's pale face munching through her cereal and remarks on it,

"You look a bit peaky dear, is it your period?"

"No mum, but I didn't sleep very well."

"Not worrying about exam results I hope. I'm sure you did your best and you can't do any better than that."

"Oh no. It's something Melissa Dean was saying to Sally Foster yesterday. You know the bother about Tom Prescott? Yes well, I overheard them saying that Annette Grayson made it all up and something about Annette's father. She always burned a torch for Mr. Prescott. She cried when he told her and Melissa off at Whitby for larking about near the cliff edge. Sally Foster was telling Melissa that her sister Bella hates staying at their house. She stays there after rehearsal on Fridays and she's scared to death of Annette's father. Says he's always touching them."

"This is yesterday you say? You realize I'll have to tell Will Metcalfe and Dad what you just told me? It will stop them bringing Tom to court if what you say is true."

"I don't care, we want our form master back."
Mandy leaves the table and is going through the door when she turns back.

" and Mum---"

"Something else?"

"Yes. Annette Grayson often has funny marks on her bust and back."

"How do you know that? Does she show you?"

"No, she tries to hide them with her towel, but when she's in the showers after P.E. and games, I've seen them."

A cold shiver of horror trickles down Kath's back.

"What kind of marks? Moles or spots you mean or birthmarks?"

"No. More like bruises on her front but those on her back and on her bum are stripes."

"Has she been in school since Monday?"

"No. She's been off since then. Can't face the rest of us I shouldn't wonder. You knew some lads from our year beat up Joe Prescott yesterday? That Rodney Needham led the others on. He's poison."

She shrugs her shoulders and screws up her face as she stands half in and half out the door.

"Do anything to cause trouble, he would. Thinks he's really clever. Well he's always been sweet on Annette but she won't have anything to do with him."

"Yes I heard about young Joe. That poor family are having a terrible time this week because of that silly girl."

Kath sits over her second cup of tea and mutters to herself.

"Perhaps the poor girl is more to be pitied than blamed."

She gazes through the window and sips her tea thoughtfully.

"This saga is going to pull the plug on some sludge I think and bring a few secrets out into the open."

Kath slips on her coat and outdoor shoes and makes her way to the Police Station to pass on her news to Will Metcalfe.

**

Tom answers the phone as he comes in from the garden at lunchtime. It's his Headmaster, Peter Finch. He rings Tom each day since his suspension to see how he is and try to cheer him up.

"How are you this morning Tom? Sergeant Metcalfe was just telling me that things look a little more hopeful for you, but wouldn't elaborate on that. Have you heard anything further?"

"Good morning Headmaster. Yes, apparently the police picked up the girl early this morning in Darlington and are interviewing her today, without her parents. Let's hope she

226

tells the truth this time. I feel sorry for her because I'm sure she's in some trouble."

"Yes, you mentioned that. Do you think she is abused in some way?"

"Yes I do. Anyway, I expect it will all come out now. Incidentally Sir, it's orchestra rehearsal this evening. Will it be correct for me to go along and help Hazel with chairs and things?"

"Of course it will. It's outside school hours although it's on school premises. With some luck, we should have you back where you belong next week. Goodbye Tom."

'They say absence makes the heart fonder and I think Sir is missing me.' Tom muses to the dead phone. He's having lunch at his mother's before painting her garage and shed and thinks he may as well go and get on with it.

**

"Now Sergeant Metcalfe, I've just had Tom Prescott's mother in here raising Cain because we're not doing anything. You've seen Mr.Grayson again and obtained the court order for us to interview his daughter without him? He seems determined we shall not see her alone. Shame we had to go over his head. There's a lot more to this than meets the eye. Has she turned up yet?"

"Yes sir. She was found in a Darlington Hostel this morning and a police car is bringing her in.."

"Is it all set for her to be interviewed today?"

"Yes, Sir. She has been examined by our physician and her report will be sent on. Everything's arranged. I feel sorry that Tom's been sweating it out this week, but Grayson held things up by being so difficult and then the girl doing a runner. Did you notice anything about that glove print Sir? It puzzled me for a bit."

"That it's the left hand you mean and the wrong way up. Yes he couldn't have been touching her on that side with that glove could he? In fact the only way you could have a print like that is from behind or do it yourself. Took me a while too. You should get her on that if she spins some more yarns. I'm sorry not to be able to do this interview but I have to get over to Richmond, I'm in court this morning. You can update me when I ring at lunchtime."

**

A small table is in the middle of an interview room at Weybury police station.

Annette Grayson is sitting one side with a Woman Police Constable next to her and Will Metcalfe on the other. There is a constable beside him operating a tape recorder and with a pen, waiting for data. The girl looks bedraggled and terrified sitting awkwardly on the wooden chair. There is a large bruise on the left side of her face and her left eye is discoloured.

Annette never dreamed she would feel this way when she imagined leaving home. Now she has made the break from her parents, she feels desolate, frightened and very alone. She slept badly and the kids at the Hostel were rough and horrible. There were two old women there too and they'd been on the bottle. Her purse was gone this morning; one of them must have seen her fall asleep and pinched it from underneath her pillow. Annette told the wardens she'd been robbed and couldn't pay, but they didn't do anything about it. The Police paid her board, but she couldn't eat any breakfast. She would be glad to tell the truth even if her father did go to prison. The thought of him made the nausea sweep over her again.

The tape recorder is running as Will says gently,

"Annette, this machine will record this interview accurately so there can be no errors and is always used now."

He looks at the poor girl before him and thinks of his own daughter.

"I know that the story you told your father wasn't the truth. Now that he's not here, can you tell me exactly what happened on Monday night and why you said those things? I know something did and the truth is better than another story."

He notes her frightened face and says in a gentle voice,

"Don't worry about the tape recorder; it's there so I can't say something you didn't tell me. If you're afraid to go home because your father will be angry, we can sort that out for you, but you must tell us the truth now."

The girl swallows hard. She wants to tell Will Metcalfe everything. It will be a relief when it's all out in the open but what if her father comes raging up here and drags her home. He would beat her to a pulp this time and God knew what else, for letting it all out. Oh God, what should she do? She says nothing, just looks at the policeman with brown puppy dog eyes and tears plopping on her hand. The woman PC pats her hand,

"You don't have to worry dear. Just tell the truth now."

"Is something bothering you Annette? You don't ever have to go home again you know unless you want to. We can find somewhere else for you to live."

"I don't want to meet my father."
The words are so quiet that Will isn't sure he's heard it them correctly.

"I can promise you that if there is good reason for your father not to take you home, we'll help you to live away from him. Does that make you feel safer?"

"I think so but he'll come looking for me wherever you put me. He's a mad-man."

"I promise that you have nothing to fear if you tell us the truth and you've done nothing wrong. Now, how about the real story?"

Annette rubs her wet nose and scrubs the tears with the back of her hand. The Police Woman passes her a box of tissues and she takes some to wipe her face. Looking uncertainly at both the woman constable and Will Metcalfe she sniffs and swallows hard, then begins in a shaky voice.

"I was in bed at nine o-clock, one of my father's rules on Mondays. He insists I'm in bed before he goes out to his meeting."

"Your mother was in the house?"

"Yes, she stays up half the night watching the telly."

"So, your father was preparing to go out and you were in bed?"

"I could hear him in the shower. Then he comes to my room."

The girl shudders at the mental picture of her father in his blue checked dressing gown that showed his skinny celery legs.

"He sits on the side of the bed. He always asks me if any boys have kissed me yet. He says he'll beat me senseless if they do. Then he grabs me and shows me how he says real men kiss girls. Ugh, it's horrible."

"Your father does this every night?"

"Yes. I knew he wouldn't forget. I had to think up some story to stop him."

"I don't understand what you're saying here Annette. You had to stop him beating you?"

"No. I didn't mind that so much. I had to stop him mauling me and making me touch him and- - and do things. I couldn't bear it any more."

"Annette, let me get this right. Your father comes into your room every night before he goes to bed? He comes in earlier on Mondays because he goes out and you have to be in bed before that. Be very sure you're telling me the truth."

The girl becomes agitated but continues in a stronger voice.

"It's the truth, he's been doing it for months. I couldn't stand it any longer."

The girl puts her arms on the table and resting her head on them, lets out her fear and misery in heartbreaking sobs.

The W.P.C puts her arm across her shoulders,

"Let it out dear. It's time for the truth now. We'll protect you when we know what really happened."

She looks at Sergeant Metcalfe over the girl's head. His face has blanched.

When the sobbing quietens Will asks,

"Did your father beat you that night Annette?"

"Yes he did."

Annette snuffles into her screwed up tissue.

"He wears a thin leather belt round his dressing gown instead of a cord and he beats me with that. I couldn't go to school the next day."

"So, he beat you because you told him a story. Is that it?"

"Yes. He went berserk. I've never seen him so mad. I was terrified. I thought he was going to kill me. I screamed at him to stop but he didn't hear me, he was so mad."

"Did your mother come up?"

"No, she's too scared of him."

"The story you told him. Was it about Tom Prescott touching you?"

"Yes. I had to tell him something quick and it was the first thing I could think of. A beating is better than—than the other. But he mauled me about even worse after that and really hurt me."

"So. Tell me truthfully Annette. At no time did Tom Prescott come into your garden or touch you in a bad way?"

"No. He wouldn't do such a thing. He's a super bloke. I never thought my father would go to the police and get him suspended. I didn't know he was put out of school till I saw it in the paper. I just had to stop my father making me do things to him and mauling me about. I'm sorry. I didn't mean to cause all this trouble."

Her voice cracks and fresh tears pour down her face. She takes more tissues and it's several moments before she can continue.

"Well, you needed help but it certainly has caused a great deal of distress to the Prescott family. What about the bikini and the hand mark? How did that get there?"

"Oh that. I did that when he went to the cricket match. I'd been watching him from the attic window. I often do. I think he's great. I always wished he was my father. They seem such a happy family doing things together.""
There's another pause while the girl blows her nose. Will Metcalfe fidgets in his chair and the WPC strokes Annette's hair.

"I'd been sunbathing and when he went, I touched the gate he'd been painting because he'd touched it. Then I wondered what it would be like if he held me and put the glove on and put my hands on my bot-- er back, pretending it was him."

"Did you want your parents to see the hand mark?"

"No. I didn't realize the paint was still wet until I took the pants off. I was going to get it off with something. I hid it in my draw."

"But you showed it to your father that night?"

"No, no I didn't. He found it. He said I must have some love letters hidden somewhere. He pulled all my things out of my drawers and threw them all over the floor. He was like a raving lunatic. That's when he saw it."

"What about the scars and marks on Mr. Prescott's back? How did you know about those?"

"I told you. I watch him through the attic window."

"You have some binoculars up in the attic then and you know how to use them?"

"Of course I do."

Annette looks embarrassed now and turns her face away, realizing she has said more than she intended.

"So, you watch Mr. Prescott with binoculars through the attic window? No wonder you know so much about him."

Will switches off the tape recorder and turns the tape over before asking,

"Why did you wait until yesterday to leave home Annette?"

241

"I couldn't go before. I was so sore I could hardly move and I had to get some cash without my father knowing. So I waited until Thursday when I felt better then went towards school and slipped back to the bank, got the money then caught the bus to Richmond. I walked around for a bit but I know a lot of people there so I caught a bus to Darlington. I'd nowhere to go where they wouldn't think to look so I went to the Hostel. It's horrible there." The tears begin to flow again and she sobs into her hands.

Will Metcalfe clears his throat and shuffles in his chair before continuing with formalities.

"Well now, the Police Doctor will need to examine you to see where you were beaten. I have to tell your parents you are safe and where

242

you are and I expect your father will be annoyed. He's at present in a cell because he caused a disturbance but will be released latertoday. We cannot allow you to go home because of your situation so, we'll arrange for you to stay overnight at least, with a family in Richmond who foster emergencies, until everything is sorted out."

"You won't send me back home will you? I couldn't bear to go through that again. I could go to my Auntie Connie's up at Waithe."

"I'm afraid that for the moment you'll be placed 'In Care' because we cannot risk your father storming round and causing unpleasantness if he knows your whereabouts."

"Oh dear. Will it be like that other place?"

"No Annette, this is an ordinary family living in a house. They just happen to be special people who give a bed to children in trouble."

He looks at the girl before him for a moment, giving her time to blow her nose again.

"Tell me, did your mother never intervene to protect you from your father bothering you?"

"Once she tried but he sent her away. He beats her up as well and after that she stayed downstairs. She used to put cream on my back if he belted me. I wanted her to tell my Auntie Connie or Meg that he mauls me about, but she just said they'd put us all in prison. I hope they do. It can't be worse than living there."

CHAPTER ELEVEN. SAFE HARBOUR

After a hasty tea, Hazel arrives at the school hall in Weyburne Comprehensive on Friday evening, in good time to help organize the stage seating for the rehearsal. With his Headmaster's permission Tom goes along, as usual, to give her a hand with the chairs. It's a strange feeling for him.

"You know Hazel, I keep looking over my shoulder to see if somebody's coming to grab me. I feel as though I'm doing something wrong, being here."

"But Mr. Finch gave his OK didn't he? I'll bet you'll really appreciate being back here again. You've missed it all haven't you?"

"I certainly have. It'll be like coming home after a long illness. I suppose you never realize how much something means to you until you lose it. Do you need any more chairs this side?"

Two girls approach Tom as he is arranging chairs. Melissa Dean begins nervously,

"Mr Prescott, can we tell you something?"

"Of course Melissa, got a problem?"

"No Sir er yes Sir. Well Sir, you know that story Annette Grayson told her father? Well, it isn't true. She made it all up."

"You don't say. How do you know this? Did she tell you?"
Sally Foster butted in with,

"No Sir. We haven't seen her because she's been off school. We know she watches you from their attic window. She told me that."

"Well thank you both for telling me this. I think the Police will find out the truth."

"Does that mean you'll be coming back to school soon Sir? We don't think much of this new teacher."

247

"Now you behave and show this new teacher how good you can be or else he will blame me for your bad manners. And I'll give you all another geography exam when I come back."

"Yes Sir."

The two girls saunter off giggling and chattering to resume unpacking their things. Leaving a very thoughtful Tom behind.

The children are drifting into the hall, lugging their various burdens. Cellos, violins, flutes, drums of different sizes, oboes, piccolos, saxophones, a huge double base, trombones and trumpets, are all manoeuvred into their positions and chairs arranged to suit. Then there is the performance of erecting the ancient music stands. Tom has to give assistance here to what should be a simple operation in the right hands, but in the hands of most of the children becomes a deckchair farce.

Hazel suddenly finds herself clasped by a pair of skinny arms and a girlie voice gabbles,

"You did it Mrs. Prescott. Oh, thank you, thank you. I don't have to stay at Aunty Wilma's. I'm going home tonight."
Turning to see little Bella Foster clinging to her middle, Hazel pats her arm,

"Did Mr. Royston fit you in his car love, I'm pleased. You'll be able to sleep in your own bed tonight."
It's like a miracle. All trace of anxiety has vanished from the child's face, her eyes shine and her smile is a joy to see. Hazel asks no questions, if Bella wants to tell her anything she'll do it in her own time. The urgency is gone.

Hazel returns to the throng and bustle. Rehearsals are always a social occasion, people who taxi the children to school have probably not met since the previous week and there is news to catch up on and lambing or haytime to discuss. People performing in the current Operatic show have to catch up on their rehearsal changes. The children themselves are meeting friends and relatives and there are secrets to divulge. The noise is deafening. Clangs and bumps, squeaks and scrapes, all the unmelodious din of an orchestra tuning up, combined with excited voices and feet, large in size and number scudding the floor.

Nick Chaplin the conductor chats to Hazel before quietly stepping up on to his podium and tapping his baton on the music stand. Immediately, there is hush. Every face turns in his direction awaiting his command.

"Give me an 'A' please Bella."

Bella plays the note and he turns to the full orchestra.

"An 'A' please everybody."

The rehearsal has begun.

During the short interval, people are milling around with coffee when Sergeant Metcalfe marches into the hall, looks round and makes a beeline for Tom. Everybody stops whatever they are doing to take notice, nudging their neighbours to make them aware of the new arrival.

"Are they arresting Tom?"

"Surely it needs two cops to do that."

"They'd never arrest him in such a public place, would they?"

251

"What's happening?"

Will touches Tom's arm and informs him in a carrying tone,

"I've been ringing you all day Tom, your Wendy said I'd find you here."

A beaming Will Metcalfe grabs his hand and shakes it vigorously.

"You're off the hook old chap. The girl confessed all at interview this afternoon. That's why I've been ringing you. We've questioned Grayson but I can't tell you any more just yet. Anyway, the main thing is, you're in the clear."

A wide-eyed Hazel is watching this encounter with avid curiosity. She runs over to the two men in time to hear the last few words.

"Will? Tom? Did I hear right? It's all over?"

Tom hugs her and dances her around as ten years drop from him,

"Yes my darling. It's all over. We're free to get on with our lives."

Nick Chaplin is standing nearby and turning to the orchestra he waves his baton and begins chanting,

"For he's a jolly good fellow, for he's a jolly good fellow."

There's an instant response and a cacophony of sound from the musicians as they play a very familiar tune.

Nick continues from his podium,

"That's wonderful news. Did everybody hear? Our Tom's in the clear."

"Wow. A poet as well as a musician. Great news Tom. We would never have believed it anyway, even if they'd sent you to prison. We knew they had the wrong chap."

Polly Baxter comes forward to wring his hand, before he is surrounded. Everybody wants to slap his shoulder, shake his hand, or just tell him they are glad for him.

Susie Smith the correspondent for the Darlington and Stockton Times says,

"I'm so pleased for you Tom. I'm just sorry that it was in the D. & S. at all, but I'll ring this news through to the Northern Echo now. It might catch the late news for tomorrow and it will certainly be in next Thursday's D & S."

Matthew Cross has the last word.

"I don't know. What bosh some newspapers do print. Sensationalism, that's what it is."